A CARPENTER AND QUINCANNON
MYSTERY

THE DANGEROUS LADIES AFFAIR

MARCIA MULLER
AND
BILL PRONZINI

THORNDIKE PRESS
A part of Gale, Cengage Learning

GALE
CENGAGE Learning

Farmington Hills, Mich • San Francisco • New York • Waterville, Maine
Meriden, Conn • Mason, Ohio • Chicago

Copyright © 2016 by Pronzini-Muller Family Trust.
Thorndike Press, a part of Gale, Cengage Learning.

Thorndike Press® Large Print Mystery.
The text of this Large Print edition is unabridged.
Other aspects of the book may vary from the original edition.
Set in 16 pt. Plantin.

LIBRARY OF CONGRESS CATALOGING-IN-PUBLICATION DATA

Names: Muller, Marcia, author. | Pronzini, Bill, author.
Title: The dangerous ladies affair / Marcia Muller and Bill Pronzini.
Description: Large print edition. | Waterville, Maine : Thorndike Press, 2017. |
  Series: A Carpenter and Quincannon mystery | Series: Thorndike Press large
  print mystery
Identifiers: LCCN 2016053160 | ISBN 9781410497291 (hardback) | ISBN 1410497291
  (hardcover)
Subjects: LCSH: Private investigators—California—San Francisco—Fiction. | Women
  detectives—California—San Francisco—Fiction. | Large type books. | BISAC:
  FICTION / Mystery & Detective / Historical. | GSAFD: Mystery fiction.
Classification: LCC PS3563.U397 D364 2017 | DDC 813/.54—dc23
LC record available at https://lccn.loc.gov/2016053160

Published in 2017 by arrangement with Tom Doherty Associates

Printed in the United States of America
1 2 3 4 5 6 7 21 20 19 18 17

For the Professor, H. C. Arbuckle III,
our #1 Texas fan

SABINA

The spokes of bicycle wheels twirled and gleamed in the sunlight as scores of riders, alone, in tandem, and in groups, sped along the network of tree-bordered paths in San Francisco's Golden Gate Park. The bloomers of the women cyclists billowed out in the wind off the nearby Pacific Ocean — flowing fabrics tight at the waist, cinched in at the knee, and adorned with varicolored flowers, stripes, and checks. Some of the gentlemen wheelers, clad in knickerbockers and white or striped jackets, steered with one hand while the other clutched a straw boater or Alpine hat to his head to keep it from being stolen by the breeze. On this crisp spring day the park was alive with the colors and motion of the cycling mania that was sweeping not only the city but also, from all reports, the rest of the country.

The park, now nearly thirty years old,

covered a thousand acres from the Panhandle on its eastern end to the Great Highway and the miles-long fence erected across the length of Ocean Beach as a barricade against wind-whipped sand. Scores of winding lanes, a wealth of trees and fragrant plantings, and numerous bridges spanning the Chain of Lakes and its streams and their tributaries made it a favorite of casual weekend cyclists as well as organized clubs. Among the most avid riders were members of the Golden Gate Ladies' Bicycle Club; known as "scorchers," they were swift and sure and ample competition for many of the men, save the daredevils who had preempted the title of "crackerjacks."

Sabina Carpenter had been participating in these Sunday GGLBC excursions for several weeks now, weather permitting, at the encouragement of her new friend Amity Wellman. She found the outings exhilarating: the speed, the wind in her hair, the challenge to her muscles, the freedom of movement. Critical comments in the press from mostly male reporters that bicycle riding was harmful to women's health, and implying that it was sexually stimulating to a dangerous degree, was stuff and nonsense. The idea of hundreds of predatory bloomer-clad women on wheels amorously descending upon crowds of timorous men amused her greatly.

She enjoyed cycling so much that she had attempted to interest her partner in Carpenter and Quincannon, Professional Detective Services, in taking part in the sport and perhaps joining one of the wheelmen's clubs. John had flatly refused. It was all well and good for ladies to go bicycle riding, he said, but he considered the men who did so to be "sissified." Which was ridiculous, of course, but God knew John had his blind spots. Well, it was probably just as well. The thought of him with his large frame and thick freebooter's beard outfitted in banded breeches, a striped jacket, and an Alpine hat, his long legs pumping furiously at the pedals of a bicycle, was somewhat ludicrous — not that she would ever have said so to him.

She had met Amity Wellman, who rode beside her this afternoon, at a woman suffrage group meeting some months ago. Amity was well known in the drive to add California as a Fourth Star to the suffragists' banner, the other three states in which women had been granted the right to vote being Wyoming, Colorado, and Utah. She was head of the most active local organization, Voting Rights for Women, and would be a delegate to the California State Woman Suffrage Convention to be held in the city in November — the focal point of a state-wide campaign for an amendment to the state constitution.

Not only was Sabina in sympathy with the cause, but she was herself an ardent suffragist. She had long considered herself to be a "New Woman," the term used to describe the modern woman who broke with the traditional role of wife and mother by working outside the home — an attitude encouraged by her late husband, Stephen, during their relatively short time together. His sudden death by an outlaw's hand outside Denver, her work as a "Pink Rose" for the Pinkerton Detective Agency, and her subsequent move to San Francisco to join forces with John had all deepened and broadened her sense of independence; as the widowed co-owner of a highly respectable business, she was free of many of the strictures imposed on single and married women alike. While she had always supported the suffrage movement, she had been kept too busy to take as active a role as she would have liked. The ever-increasing number of women throughout the city and state who had joined the struggle, and the emergence of outspoken leaders such as Amity Wellman, had convinced Sabina that she needed to give more of herself to the cause.

While Amity had the full backing of her wealthy husband, Burton Wellman, a noted buyer and seller of Spanish and other valuable antiques, she had been ridiculed and angrily denounced by the misogynist elements within the city's population. As had many of her sisters, Sabina among them — in her case from hidebound clients, business associates, and casual acquaintances. Thank heaven John wasn't one of them, else their professional association as well as their budding personal relationship would have suffered. Despite an occasional poorly considered remark, he genuinely respected and admired women, valued those with the drive to forge ahead in a world still heavily weighted against their success.

Riding beside her now, Amity slowed, raised a hand to indicate a rest stop, and veered off the path as they neared one of the many animal habitats that dotted the park, this one of bison, deer, and elk. Sabina followed suit. They laid their safety cycles on the grass and went to sit on a nearby stone bench. Sabina was a trifle winded, Amity not at all, for she had been riding regularly for many years. She was a few years older than Sabina's thirty-two and in

11

splendid physical condition — tall, willowy, long legged, and narrow hipped, with a wealth of taffy-colored hair that she wore in braided coils atop her head.

She had been unusually quiet today. There were dark smudges under her eyes, testimony to a lack of sleep, and her mouth was a taut line instead of stretched into its usual tip-tilted smile. This prompted Sabina to ask, "Amity, is something troubling you?"

"Yes, there is. I've been trying to decide if I should discuss it with you, ask for your professional advice. I know it's an imposition —"

"Not at all. Is it serious?"

"It may be. I just don't know."

"Tell me about it."

"I'll do better than that — I'll show you."

From the pocket of her bloomers Amity extracted a folded envelope, which she handed to Sabina. It was of heavy vellum, as were the two sheets of stationery folded inside. The envelope bore nothing more than Amity's name, so it had not come by post. The black-ink letters on both it and the enclosures had been printed by the same practiced hand, the words so perfectly aligned that they might have been formed with the aid of a ruler.

The first sheet contained half a dozen lines:

Beware of false prophets, which come to you in sheep's clothing, but inwardly they are ravening wolves. You have trespassed upon the Lord's word. Repent and beg His forgiveness, NOW, or you will suffer the full measure of His wrath.

And on the second sheet:

And the devil that deceived them was cast into the lake of fire and brimstone, where the beast and the false prophet are, and shall be tormented day and night for ever and ever. DO NOT FAIL TO TAKE HEED OR ELSE!

"When did you receive these?" Sabina asked, frowning.

"The ravening-wolves one two days ago, the other yesterday morning. There was another of the same sort four days ago that I tore up and threw away. Lord knows I've had my share of crank messages since I assumed the leadership role in Voting Rights for Women, and these may well be more of the same. But this last one . . . Perhaps I'm overreacting, but I can't help feeling it and the others might constitute a serious threat."

"Do you have any idea who wrote them?"

Amity hesitated for a moment before answering. "The penmanship isn't familiar," she said, which didn't exactly answer Sabina's question.

"How and where were they delivered?"

"To my home. Slipped through the mail slot."

"What did the first message say?"

"Similar to the others — a warning that I would burn in hell for flouting the Lord's command about submitting to the dominant male. I know our movement disturbs a number of men, and some women as well, but . . ."

"Are there any who have been particularly virulent in their opposition to your work?"

"No remonstrants," Amity said, using the colloquial term for those old-line (Sabina preferred "mossbacked") members of their sex who belonged to the Woman Anti-Suffrage Association. "But there is one male I've clashed with on more than one occasion."

"And he is?"

"Nathaniel Dobbs."

Dobbs, the city's former Water Department commissioner, was head of the Solidarity Party, a quasi-political group known as the "Antis" for their determined and outspoken stand against anything of a progressive nature. The suffrage movement in general and Voting Rights for Women in particular were their primary targets, though as far as Sabina knew, Dobbs and his followers had thus far restricted their opposition to the picketing of suffrage rallies, bombastic verbal assaults, and inflammatory pamphlets and newspaper articles.

"Has Dobbs ever threatened you?" she asked.

"No. But he's been unpleasant and insulting when our paths have crossed. He hates and fears women to an alarming degree."

"Capable of violence, then?"

"Perhaps. I simply don't know."

"Did you show the notes to your husband?"

"No. Burton has been away on one of his buying trips, in Sacramento and the northern Mother Lode this time, for more than a month. He won't be back for another week or so."

"So you're alone in the house."

"Yes, except for Kamiko and our cook."

Kamiko was the young Japanese woman who, as an abandoned immigrant child, had been given shelter by the Wellmans and become their ward. Now that she had matured, she acted as their housekeeper —

15

by her choice, for Amity and Burton considered her their daughter, not a servant. She was well named, Amity had said once, for the English translation of Kamiko was "superior child."

"Does she know about the messages?" Sabina asked.

"Yes. I showed this one to her and told her about the others." Amity paused, nibbling at her full lower lip. "She's afraid for me. And of something else, too, perhaps."

"Why do you say that?"

"I had the feeling she was keeping something from me, some sort of secret concern."

"As if she might suspect the identity of the message writer?"

"I can't imagine how she could," Amity said. "I questioned her and she denied it."

Sabina had met Kamiko on the two occasions she'd accepted invitations to the Wellman home. The Japanese girl, while somewhat reserved, had been pleasant and friendly — not at all the so-called inscrutable Oriental. It was difficult to believe that she would withhold vital information from the woman who had raised her and whom she adored. Or, for that matter, that she or any member of her mostly Buddhist race could be responsible for threatening notes composed of dire biblical phrases.

16

"This is just a thought," Sabina said. "Does Kamiko have a swain, a Caucasian of whom you don't approve and who dislikes you as a result?"

"No. If she did have a swain, I would know it. And it's my belief she would neither keep company with nor marry a Caucasian. Despite her Westernized upbringing, she is still very much a woman of her race."

Sabina asked, "Is there anyone other than Nathaniel Dobbs, anyone at all, who might want to harm you? Someone affiliated with the Liquor Dealers League, for instance?"

Amity shifted her gaze away from Sabina to another group of cyclists flashing by. It was several seconds, with her eyes still averted, before she said, "No. Not where the movement is concerned."

"For some other reason, then?"

"No."

"Are you sure?"

"I'm sure."

She's lying. I wonder why. Something — a name, a dispute, an incident she's afraid or unwilling to reveal? Kamiko isn't the only one with a secret, it seems.

"What do you think, Sabina? *Am* I overreacting? Or should I be concerned?"

"Threatening notes are always a cause for

17

concern. You might bring them to the attention of the police —"

"Oh, Lord, no. Policemen in general hold our cause in low regard; you know that. They would merely dismiss me as a hysterical female and do nothing."

Sabina had no great liking for or trust in San Francisco's constabulary herself, though she wasn't quite as vehemently scornful in her feelings as John, who considered all but a select handful of police officials to be incompetent, corrupt, or both. In this case, Amity was no doubt right to want to avoid dealing with them.

"Is there anything *you* can do, Sabina? Any way you can find out who wrote the notes and whether or not the threats are genuine?"

"I could try, but —"

"I'd pay you, of course. Your usual fee for such investigations."

"That's not an issue. The fact is, attempting to track down anonymous notes with no more information than you've given me would be an extremely difficult undertaking. I could speak to Dobbs, but it would serve no real purpose. Even if he's guilty, he would simply deny it."

"Then there's nothing to be done?"

"I didn't say that. I could arrange to have

an operative stay with you until your husband returns —"

"A male operative? No, that wouldn't do."

"Not a male, a woman," Sabina said. "A highly competent former police matron who has done excellent work for our agency in the past."

Amity considered this, nibbling again at her lower lip. Then, slowly, she shook her head. "How would it look to our sisters, to our opponents, if I were to have a bodyguard staying in my home and accompanying me to meetings and such? No, that won't do, either. I'm a New Woman, and I won't damage my reputation or the movement's by acting like a weak sister in public or private. I'm not all that afraid for my life."

"I never doubted your strength or your courage, Amity."

"Thank you. So there is nothing else you can recommend?"

"Other than what we've discussed, and for you to be on your guard whether or not there are any more of these messages, I'm afraid there isn't." Sabina paused. "Well, that's not quite true," she said then. "There is one thing I can do, not as a detective but as a friend."

"Yes?"

"Have a private talk with Kamiko, if you

have no objection."

"No, no objection. But what good would it do? She'd be even less likely to confide in you, a relative stranger."

"That's probably true, but it couldn't hurt to try. I'm a different sort of authority figure and I have certain professional powers of persuasion. You mentioned that you'll be busy tomorrow and the rest of the week preparing for Friday evening's benefit rally in Union Square. I could drop by your house while you're away —"

"I have a better idea," Amity said. "If you have no engagement planned for this evening, why not come back home with me and we'll have dinner together? I'll tell Kamiko that I've confided in you, then make some excuse to leave you and her alone together."

Sabina had no plans and saw no reason to refuse the invitation. When Amity added, "Please say yes. I'd be grateful for your company tonight," she accepted.

Amity stood then and went to lift her bicycle from the grass. Following suit with hers, Sabina asked, "Shall we try to find the rest of our group?"

"No, let's return directly to the club-house," Amity said. "I seem to have lost my enthusiasm for any more pleasure cycling today. Frankly, what I'd very much prefer,

20

and the sooner the better, is a large glass of Burton's amontillado."

2

SABINA

The clubhouse rented by the Golden Gate
Ladies' Bicycle Club was on Clayton Street
near the Panhandle. They left their bicycles
there, washed, and changed clothes. Although the Wellmans owned a private carriage, Amity preferred to take public transportation whenever possible. A pair of
trolleys and a cable car, therefore, delivered
her and Sabina to the Wellman home on
Telegraph Hill.

The house, a two-story gingerbread-
festooned pile set back from the sloping
street behind a fence of filigreed black iron
pickets, was not the largest in the neighborhood, but it was among the best maintained
and most attractively landscaped. Flower
beds and flowering shrubs, greensward, and
rows of Australian cypress filled its front
and side yards. The front gate was not kept
locked, and the nearest electric streetlamp

was some distance away; it wouldn't have been difficult, Sabina thought, for whoever had delivered the threatening notes to have slipped in and out unseen between midnight and dawn.

Kamiko appeared before they reached the front entrance, as if she had been watching for her guardian's return. She was a petite girl, lightly brown skinned, her long black hair piled high and fastened with ivory combs. Her facial features and body structure were delicate, but her stature and slenderness concealed a surprising strength; Sabina had witnessed her shoulder with little effort a full crate of statuettes Burton Wellman had sent to their home. As she had on Sabina's previous visits, Kamiko wore a traditional Japanese kimono, which she preferred to Western clothes while at home, the garment rather plainly decorated and tied with a red *obi*.

She welcomed them with bows and smiles, asked in her flawless English if they had had a pleasant day and conducted them into the parlor. There was nothing discerningly different in the way she looked at or spoke to Amity; Kamiko's usual serenity seemed undisturbed. If she was in fact frightened for her guardian and in possession of some sort of secret knowledge about the notes, she kept it well hidden.

"Mrs. Carpenter will be dining with us this evening, Kamiko," Amity said.

"I shall inform the cook. Will you have tea now?"

"No. Sherry for me. Sabina?"

"The same."

"Mr. Wellman's amontillado, please."

Kamiko bowed again and hurried off, her slippers whispering on the hardwood floor.

The parlor was furnished, as was the rest of the house — Sabina had been given a tour on her first visit — in the type of expensive Spanish antiques Burton Wellman specialized in. Here there were several early-century *estrado* chairs, a sofa with damask cushions, a large central table, corner tables, paintings of California missions on the walls, and damask curtains on the windows. The furnishings were all attractive, but much too dark for Sabina's taste; the only color in the room was provided by Burton's collection of antique weaponry — a bejeweled Spanish dagger, a pair of matching Polish blunderbuss pistols, a Malay kris, a Japanese double-edged *kaiken* with a finely carved ivory handle and matching scabbard, a medieval Scottish ax, and many more large and small weapons from around the globe. Amity had confessed that she, too, was less than fond of the motif — and of the weaponry, for that matter — but since she spent little enough time here and devoted her attention to more important matters, she deferred to her husband's preferences.

Burton's vintage amontillado sherry, which Kamiko served in ornate tulip glasses, was excellent. While Sabina and Amity sipped it in front of a blazing log fire, they discussed the proposed amendment to the state constitution giving California women the right to vote, and the opposition to it.

The primary and most formidable opponent was the Liquor Dealers League, an organization composed of the producers, proprietors, and consumers of alcoholic beverages. Less powerful but nonetheless active were Nathaniel Dobbs' Solidarity Party, the traitorous (Amity's word) remonstrants, and assorted small groups with similarly old-fashioned views. They wrote letters to the newspapers and gave speeches direly warning that women would attempt to serve as soldiers, sailors, policemen, and firemen and elect themselves to executive offices and judgeships, thus threatening male livelihoods and male dominance. Dobbs, for one, had also ridiculously accused men who supported woman suffrage

25

of lacking in both wisdom and masculinity.

There was no question that the former water commissioner was a misogynistic buffoon, but Sabina still had difficulty believing he would actually commit or sanction bodily harm. Everything she knew or had heard of the man indicated he was full of a great deal of smoke (among other things) but no real fire. One of the many things she'd learned during her years as a detective, however, was never to take anyone or anything at face value.

Dinner was served at a long, parquetry-top refectory table in the spacious dining room. A succulent shrimp and crab cocktail, rare roast beef, potatoes and vegetables, and chocolate custard for dessert. Sabina, ravenous after the afternoon's exercise and two glasses of amontillado, ate lustily. Her appetite and capacity rivaled John's despite the difference in their sizes, and her metabolism and active lifestyle were such that she never gained an ounce. She weighed the same as she had when she and Stephen were married in her native Chicago.

Afterward she and Amity returned to the parlor. Amity declined Kamiko's offer of coffee, saying that she felt the need of some fresh air and would go for a walk in the garden.

"Are you certain this is wise, Amity-san?" the girl said. "It is very cold tonight."

"Not so cold, and I'll bundle up. Would you care to join me, Sabina?"

The invitation wasn't genuine; this was the excuse they'd decided upon to give Sabina the opportunity to speak to Kamiko alone. "Thanks, no. I believe I'll have coffee here by the fire."

When the girl had gone out, Amity asked, "How much time do you think you'll need?"

"No more than a few minutes to gain her confidence, if I can."

"I'll be surprised if you do." Her friend put on a warm lambs wool coat and went out through a pair of louvered doors into the side garden.

Kamiko brought the coffee on a silver tray. As she set it down, Sabina said, "Please sit for a moment, Kamiko. I'd like to have a few words with you."

"As you wish, Mrs. Carpenter." Obediently the girl sat on one of the *estrado* chairs, folding her hands in her lap.

"Your guardian and I had a talk at the park this afternoon," Sabina began. "She showed me the warning notes she has received."

Kamiko nodded, her almond-shaped eyes grave. "Yes. I was shown them as well."

27

"Do you feel the threats should be taken seriously?"

"No threat to one's safety should be ignored or dismissed."

"That doesn't quite answer my question. Is it your opinion that her life is in danger?"

"I do not know. I pray not."

"Do you have any idea who wrote the notes?"

There was the slightest hesitation before Kamiko said, "No. The cause Amity-san struggles for has made her many enemies."

"Is her cause one you also believe in?"

"Such beliefs are not of my culture."

"So you don't support women's suffrage, women's emancipation."

"I did not say that. Amity-san is much wiser than I. I would not presume to dispute her principles."

"Do you know of any other enemies who might wish to do her harm?"

". . . I do not." The hesitation was longer this time.

"Someone not connected with the suffrage movement with whom she's had trouble of any kind?"

"It is not my place to pry into the affairs of my elders."

Evasions and circumlocutions. Sabina felt as Amity did: Kamiko, for whatever reason, was keeping some sort of secret to herself.

"You are a detective, Mrs. Carpenter," the girl said. "May I ask if Amity-san has engaged you professionally?"

"We've discussed it. If I do investigate, I'll need as much information as possible. You will cooperate, won't you?"

"*Hai.* Of course."

"Tell me everything you know, no matter how little it might be. And above all, tell me no lies."

"I do not lie."

"Withholding important information is a form of lying and lying is a sin. You understand that, don't you?"

"Yes. I understand."

Sabina sharpened her voice, darkened her expression. "By committing such a sin, Kamiko, you are doing a serious disservice to the woman you love and respect. Why? What is it you know or suspect that you're afraid to tell?"

"I am not afraid. I —"

From outside there was a sudden terrified outcry. An instant later a second noise erupted, this one the unmistakable report of a pistol.

As swiftly as Sabina grabbed her bag and surged to her feet, Kamiko reached the louvered doors and plunged out into the

29

garden ahead of her. Small oil lanterns lit the side terrace; thin shafts of pallid moonlight slanted through the cloud cover overhead to illuminate portions of the garden. The Japanese girl must have had the night vision of a cat; crying her guardian's name, she raced straight ahead toward where an indistinct figure — Amity, judging by the bulk and light color of her coat — was struggling to rise from one of the cinder paths. In the next moment Sabina caught a glimpse of a shadow-shape outfitted in dark clothing running away among the tall Australian cypress. Her automatic reaction was to pursue; without hesitation she plunged ahead in that direction, yanking her Remington derringer from her bag as she ran.

The unfamiliar grounds hampered her; shrubbery branches caught at her shirtwaist and skirt, and twice in patches of grass untouched by moonlight she stumbled, the second time into a cypress trunk that fetched her a glancing blow on the left shoulder. Somewhere in the clotted dark ahead she heard thrashing movements, then a flat clanking sound, then nothing but her own accelerated breathing.

By the time she emerged into the front yard, the fleeing intruder had vanished. The gate in the iron picket fence stood open —

the clanking sound she'd heard as he ran through. She raced ahead to the gate, stood swiveling her head in both directions along the street. No conveyance was parked or moving in this block, and the tree-shadowed sidewalks appeared empty.

Turning, she slipped the Remington back into her bag. Her eyes had adjusted enough to the darkness for her to make out a cinder path that closely paralleled the house; she followed it to the side terrace, hurrying as much as could. Amity and Kamiko stood together at its edge, their faces illuminated by parlor and lantern light, the girl's arm wrapped protectively around her guardian's waist.

"I'm not hurt," Amity said shakily when Sabina joined them. "The shot missed me. The assailant — ?"

"Gone before I could catch up. Did you have a clear look at whoever it was?"

"No. Too dark. Just the shape of him when he appeared from behind one of the trees. That's when I screamed and he fired at me."

"It *was* a man, then."

"I'm not sure. Dressed all in black, a cap pulled down low . . . it could have been a woman. My God, yes, it could."

There was something about the way Amity spoke that last sentence that captured

31

Sabina's attention. But Kamiko was saying, "We must go inside, Amity-san," in worried tones. "You must have the fire and hot tea to warm you."

"The fire, yes, but no tea. A large glass of brandy instead."

The girl insisted on escorting her into the house, though Amity was clearly able to walk without aid. Inside, Kamiko helped her off with her coat, saw to it that she was settled in front of the fire, then hurried out.

When Sabina sat down next to her, Amity said, her voice still a trifle tremulous, "I expect we know now that those threatening notes were genuine. Someone wants me dead."

"You're certain the shot was fired straight at you?"

"Yes. Why would you think — Oh. Another, harsher warning?"

"It's possible."

"I doubt it. That pistol was aimed straight at me. The bullet came so close I felt the wind of its passage."

Kamiko returned just then, bearing a large snifter of brandy on the silver tray. She seemed reluctant to leave after serving it. She hovered, adding a log to the fire and then stoking the blaze, until Amity said, "That will be all for now, Kamiko. I'd like to speak to Sabina in private."

"As you wish, Amity-san." A bow, and the girl was gone.

"I know you didn't have much time alone with her," Amity said, "but were you able to find out anything?"

"Nothing definite. Only enough to agree with you that she is keeping something to herself."

"I just don't see how it can be important. Kamiko is devoted to me. If she knows or suspects who is behind all this devilment, she would have said so by now."

Sabina said, "Kamiko isn't the only one with secrets."

Amity had been staring into the fire. Now she turned her head to look at Sabina. "You think I am?"

"I do. I had that impression in the park, and again outside just now when you said your assailant might well be a woman. You made no mention this afternoon of trouble with anyone of our sex."

Amity started to speak, then once more shifted her gaze to the fire.

"Are you going to confide in me or not?"

"Very well." The response came after several seconds of silence and then after a heavy sigh. "One person, yes. Possibly two."

"Who and why?"

Instead of answering the questions directly, Amity said, "This is difficult for me to admit, but . . . three weeks ago I made a very foolish mistake. Burton travels so much, and I was feeling lonely and neglected. In a moment of weakness . . . well, to my everlasting regret I allowed myself to briefly become involved with another man, a married man."

Sabina managed to conceal the mild surprise she felt. "I see."

"Please don't think too harshly of me, Sabina."

"I don't. I'm not judgmental. The affair is over now, I take it."

Amity faced her again. "As of last week."

"Does Kamiko know?"

"Of course not. I pray neither she nor Burton finds out. You're the first person I've told."

"Who is the man?"

"Fenton Egan. One of the partners in Egan and Bradford, the tea and spice importers. A customer of Burton's, which is how I met him. Very good-looking, very superficially charming. And very unpleasant when things don't go his way." Amity's mouth quirked sardonically. "Or when he finds himself caught between Scylla and Charybdis."

"He was upset when you ended the affair?"

"I wasn't the one who ended it. At least not on my own initiative, though I soon would have."

"He did, then."

"No, his wife, Prudence, found out about us — I don't know how; she wouldn't say. She also knew about a letter, an indiscreet letter, Fenton wrote me at the height of our . . . well, passion."

"The usual sort of steamy love letter?"

"Yes and no. It said he fancied himself in love with me, and hinted that he wouldn't be averse to making our relationship permanent. He may have been serious at the time. More likely it was pretense, a sly attempt to prolong the affair."

"Do you still have this letter?"

"Lord, no. I burnt it in the fireplace."

"So it was with certain knowledge that Prudence Egan confronted you."

"The kind of knowledge that couldn't be refuted by lies or evasions, yes, even if I'd been so inclined. She came here. Kamiko had taken the buggy out marketing, thank God. The woman was furious . . . an ugly scene."

"Did she threaten you?"

"With dire consequences unless I ended

the affair immediately. Which I did."

"How long ago was this?"

"Five days."

"The day before the first threatening message was delivered."

"Yes."

"Have you had any dealings with her since then?"

"No. None."

"Five days is a long time to nurse a violent grudge."

"I know. But she's the brooding type. Jealous, possessive, afraid of losing the privilege that marriage to a wealthy man provides."

"Did you tell your lover about the confrontation?"

"Yes."

"How did he react?"

Amity winced at the memory. "He was angry, too, but it was a cold, vindictive anger — at me for 'leading him on and then throwing him over,' as he put it, and at his wife for daring to interfere in his affairs. He pretends to have great respect for women and women's rights, but he doesn't — he cares only about himself. I should have seen through that façade of his before I let him seduce me, but fool that I am, I didn't. He masked it so well."

"Did *he* threaten you in any way?"

"Not with physical harm, though he's probably capable of it. He intimated he might let Burton know about the affair without naming himself as the man involved."

"Would he actually do that, do you think?"

"He might have in the heat of the moment, out of pure spite, if Burton hadn't been away. He may still, though I doubt it."

"Have you had any contact with him since?"

"Absolutely not. Nor will I ever again if I can avoid it."

"Is there anything more you haven't told me?" Sabina asked. "Anyone else who might have cause, real or imagined, to want you dead?"

"No. I swear there isn't. Fenton was my first and last affair; I swear that, too. I've learned my lesson, no matter what the consequences may be."

"There may not be any further consequences."

"I pray not, but — Sabina? Have you changed your mind? Will you agree to investigate after all?"

Sabina didn't need to reconsider. After what had happened here tonight, how could she say anything but yes?

3

QUINCANNON

The Woolworth National Bank, on Montgomery Street in the heart of the Financial District, was neither the oldest nor the largest in San Francisco, but it had a reputation as favorable as any in the community. As did its president, Titus Wrixton, a man of some wealth and social prominence. This being the case, Quincannon was mildly surprised to receive a Monday-morning telephone call from one of the bank's underlings requesting an audience with Mr. Wrixton at his, Quincannon's, earliest convenience. No direct reason for the request was given, other than the fact that it concerned a matter of some urgency.

Quincannon, his interest piqued as much by the prospect of a substantial fee as by the unknown nature of the request, readily agreed to a one o'clock meeting in the banker's office. This allowed him time to make inroads on the backlog of bills, invoices, and other documents piled on his desk — a necessary if odious task that befell him since Sabina was not present. She had, however, been to the office before his arrival. It was she who had piled the paperwork on his desk blotter, topping it with a note in her neat hand:

I have a new case that likely will keep me busy for some time. Details when next I see you. Your turn to attend to the monthly necessities. No excuses!

S.

The prospect of dealing with "the monthly necessities" displeased him, but it was more than offset by the acceptance of not one but two new cases to begin the week; separate investigations meant separate fees to swell the agency's bank account. He hoped Sabina's client was likewise a person of means, not one of the indigent types she was sometimes inclined to succor. Altruism was all well and good, but it did not pay the bills. Well, he would find out soon enough. About her new case and Banker Wrixton's problem, both.

When Quincannon finished as much of the blasted paperwork as he could bear, he closed up the office and hied himself to Hoolihan's Saloon on Second Street, his favorite watering hole during his drinking days. Hoolihan's also provided the best free lunch in the city, and he partook liberally of it as usual. It was two minutes shy of the appointed hour of one o'clock when he walked into the Woolworth National Bank. He identified himself to one of the officers and was immediately shown into the president's private sanctum.

Titus Wrixton was a well-fed gent of some fifty years, with puffy muttonchop whiskers and florid features. His rather nervous manner, Quincannon judged, was not normal with him, but the result of whatever difficulty had led him to seek the services of a private investigator. Wrixton's attire, like his office, was conservative, his handshake brief and slightly moist.

"Thank you for agreeing to see me, Mr. Quincannon, and for arriving so promptly. Please. Sit down." He indicated a burgundy-colored leather chair, then a humidor atop his massive mahogany desk. "Cigar?"

"No thanks, sir. I'm strictly a pipe man."

"Ah, well then, feel free to smoke yours if you like." Wrixton waited until Quincannon sat, then deposited himself in a large padded armchair behind the desk, pooched out his cheeks, said again, "Well then," pooched his cheeks a second time, and fell silent.

Quincannon, having removed his derby, adjusted the crease in one leg of his trousers and then crossed his legs and set the hat on his knee. It was warm in the darkly wood-paneled room, but he kept his navy-blue sack coat buttoned. He wore a flowered waistcoat today, as was his wont on occasion, and this was no place to display a handsome but somewhat gaudy white silk garment adorned with red and yellow rosebuds.

He said, "I take it you asked me here for a professional consultation, Mr. Wrixton?"

"Correct. Your profession, that is to say, not mine." Pooch. "I don't quite know how to begin. It's, ah, a matter of some delicacy that demands considerable discretion."

"Rest assured, sir, that Carpenter and Quincannon, Professional Detective Services, is the soul of discretion in all matters."

"Yes, so I've been told. That is why I chose you."

"Is your problem connected with the bank?"

Another pooch, an evidently habitual trick that gave Wrixton the unflattering look of a large, red-faced rodent. "No. No, ah, it's personal."

"I see. And its nature?"

Wrixton cleared his throat and then spat the word "Extortion" as if expectorating phlegm.

"Someone is attempting to extort money from you?"

"Yes. But it's more than just an attempt."

"You've already paid?"

"Once, yes."

"May I ask how much?"

"Five thousand dollars."

Quincannon raised a bushy eyebrow. "That's quite a lot of money."

"My God, yes."

"And now there has been a second demand?"

"Last evening. For another five thousand." Angry indignation wiggled its way through Wrixton's nervousness. "I can't . . . I won't pay it. Once bitten, twice shy. The scoundrel will only keep demanding more and more."

"Blackmailers usually do," Quincannon agreed. "It is blackmail, I take it? This individual has knowledge that might be harmful to you?"

"To me personally, and to my position here at the bank."

"Of a criminal nature?"

"Criminal? Good Lord, no! I am an honest man, sir, an honest banker."

As honest as any banker in this or other communities, Quincannon thought sardonically. "I have no doubt of that, sir. What is it, then, that you're being blackmailed for?"

"Do you need to know that?"

"It would be helpful to have your complete confidence."

"But knowing the reason isn't necessary in order for you to agree to provide assistance?"

"Not if it has no direct bearing on my investigation."

"I don't see how it could. You'll respect my right not to divulge the reason, then?"

"As you wish," Quincannon said.

"There is one very important thing you do need to know." The banker paused, wincing as if struck by a sudden pang, and put his hand to his mouth to cover a faintly audible belch. He excused himself, saying, "I suffer from dyspepsia." He produced a vial from his coat pocket, chewed and swallowed two of the tablets it contained, then plucked out and consumed a third.

"You were saying, Mr. Wrixton?"

"Eh?"

"That there is something important I need to know."

"Yes. Yes. The blackmailer has, ah, certain

items of mine in his possession. You must make every possible effort to obtain them and return them to me."

"And these items are?"

". . . Letters. Private letters."

"Written by you?"

"Yes. Once you have the letters, I must ask you not to read any of them. It would be quite, um, quite . . ."

The word he couldn't quite bring himself to say, Quincannon thought, was "embarrassing." A guess as to the nature of the letters was not difficult to make. Given Wrixton's age, the fact that he had a prim socialite wife and a married daughter with two children, and the guilty flush that now stained his cheeks, his transgression likely involved a young and perhaps less than respectable member of the opposite sex. In any case, the banker had shown poor judgment in paying the first five-thousand-dollar demand and good judgment in turning to Quincannon to put an end to the bloodletting once the second demand was made. Which made Wrixton only half a fool.

"Do you agree, on your word of honor?" Wrixton asked.

"I do, though you realize I'll need to identify the letters as yours."

"That won't require reading them."

44

Pooch. "They were written on stationery that bears my letterhead."

Quincannon revised his opinion of the banker. Not half but three-quarters a fool. "How do you suppose these letters came into the blackmailer's possession?" he asked.

"I haven't a clue. Not a clue."

"How were his demands made? In person, by message?"

"By message, both of them. Here at the bank."

"Was the handwriting at all familiar?"

"No."

"So you have no idea who the blackmailer is."

"None. The man I paid the five thousand to was an emissary, or so he claimed."

"You'd never seen him before?"

"Never."

"Describe him."

"Hooked nose, sallow complexion. Rather short."

"Age?"

"In the middle forties."

"Where did the payment take place?"

"In the bar parlor of the Hotel Grant."

"And the second payment? It's to be made in the same location?"

"Yes."

All to the good. A public meeting place

should make Quincannon's task that much easier. "When?" he asked.

"Tonight, at nine o'clock," Wrixton said. "I'm to bring the money in a satchel, as I did the first time — small greenbacks, none larger than a fifty — and wait alone in a booth until the so-called emissary arrives." He covered another belch and pooched again before continuing. "Do you advise that I keep the appointment?"

"By all means."

"With the money?"

"Did he examine the first payment before leaving with it?"

"Oh, yes. Carefully, to make sure it was all there."

"Then you'll bring the full amount this time as well," Quincannon said. "And when the man comes to claim it, you're to do or say nothing that will arouse his suspicions."

"You'll be there?"

"I will. But you're not to acknowledge my presence in any way."

"What do you intend to do?"

"Observe unobtrusively, and follow him when he leaves."

"And then?"

"That depends. How would you prefer the matter handled?"

"Why, if he's not the blackmailer, find out

46

who is and stop the scoundrel from harassing me. After retrieving the letters, of course."

"By turning him over to the police?"

"No! My name must be kept out of this at all costs."

Easier said than done, Quincannon thought.

Wrixton said, "There must be some, ah, other way for you to deal with his sort."

"I am not an assassin, Mr. Wrixton."

The banker looked horrified. "No, no, certainly not. Force, coercion . . . those are methods you employ, surely?"

"When the situation calls for it," Quincannon said. He fluffed his freebooter's whiskers. "In which case, as I'm sure you realize, my fee will be substantially higher than our usual rate."

"The amount of your fee," Wrixton said resolutely, "is not and will not be an issue if you succeed in retrieving and returning my letters. Especially that, sir. Especially that."

Once more Quincannon revised his opinion of Titus Wrixton, upward this time. The banker might be three-quarters a fool, but he was also smart enough and desperate enough to accept the fact that hiring the best detective in the city, if not in the entire western United States, required compensation commensurate with said detective's substantial talents.

The agency offices were still closed, Sabina not having returned during his absence. It was a bit stuffy in there on this warm April afternoon, but he did not open any of the windows. The reason being that the faint scent of Sabina's favorite sandalwood perfume continued to linger in the air, a scent that never failed to stir his Scot's blood.

Just a few whiffs invariably brought back memories of their recent social engagements, the closeness that had begun to develop between them after five years of having his persistent attempts to establish a personal as well as professional relationship fended off. Finally — finally! — he had convinced her that his intentions were honorable and she had relented in her stand against fraternization and permitted him to keep company with her away from the office.

Evenings at the symphony, the opera, the Stage Door Theater; dinners at the Tadich Grill, the Poodle Dog, and other of the city's better restaurants; weekend carriage rides in Golden Gate Park. Thus far these outings were all she had permitted except for chaste good-night kisses, not that he had attempted any additional liberties. And thus far the kisses were enough for him, though they and the promise that lay behind them, the closeness of her slender body and the tantalizing scent of her perfume, disturbed his rest on those nights. She was a desirable woman in the prime of her life, she had been a widow for eight years now, and so far as he knew she had remained celibate since the tragic death of her husband. She was passionate in her professional pursuits; surely passion of the earthy physical variety lay dammed and dormant inside her. Someday. Ah, someday . . .

Such thoughts made him feel like a lovesick fool. Which he supposed he was, confound it. Love, by Godfrey, was not all joy and sweet yearning; it could be, and often was, a blasted nuisance. Yes, and bad for a man's digestion as well as his peace of mind. He banished the thoughts by opening the windows behind Sabina's desk and banishing her lingering scent. Then he sighed and sat down to attack the remaining paperwork.

4

SABINA

The task facing her was daunting. On the surface it seemed unlikely that either Fenton or Prudence Egan had sufficient cause to threaten and then attempt to take Amity Wellman's life, yet Sabina knew from experience that some people possessed hidden demons that caused them to act irrationally and violently. One of the Egans could be so afflicted. So could Nathaniel Dobbs or a member of the Liquor Dealers League or any other virulent opponent of woman suffrage. So could another individual Amity had offended in some way connected or unconnected to her work, perhaps without even knowing it. And it did not have to be the person who hated her enough to want her dead who had fired the shot last night; it could have been the botched work of a hired assassin.

Despite the difficulty, there were steps

Sabina could take to try to identify the culprit. And to see that Amity was protected from harm in the process. The first of these, early on Monday morning, was a visit to the Hyde Street home of Elizabeth Petrie.

The one condition Sabina had placed on her willingness to investigate was that her friend agree to the company of an unobtrusive bodyguard. Amity had reluctantly done so. If Sabina was fortunate, Elizabeth would become that bodyguard.

The former police matron, a graying widow in her middle forties with a deceptively placid exterior that concealed a sharp wit and a tough-minded, uncompromising nature, was home and pleased to see her. Elizabeth's primary profession was quilting, which she had undertaken after her police inspector husband, Oliver, was implicated in a corruption scandal and sent to prison; not long after his release, he had resumed his heavy-drinking ways and died of acute alcoholism. The scandal had cost her her matron's job, but police work was in her blood and she eagerly supplemented her income by working with the city's various private investigative agencies whenever a woman operative was needed. She particularly admired Sabina, the only member of her sex to forge a successful career in a business dominated by men; they had become friends as well as occasional professional associates.

As always — except when she was otherwise engaged, which she wasn't at present — Elizabeth readily agreed to undertake the new assignment. She was even more enthusiastic in this case because of the subject's identity. "I know Mrs. Wellman by reputation," she said. "An admirable lady, to be working as hard as she does for the rights of women. I'll do everything in my power to keep her safe."

Amity had insisted that no public mention be made of her being in the care of a bodyguard; she and Sabina agreed that the operative was to adopt the guise of an old friend and contributor of time and money to the suffrage movement, who had recently moved to San Francisco and been invited as a temporary houseguest. Elizabeth had no problem with this. She would contact Amity right away at the Parrot Street headquarters of Voting Rights for Women and arrange with her to move into the Wellmans' home this evening.

After leaving Elizabeth, Sabina considered paying a call on her cousin, Callie French, at the Van Ness Avenue residence she shared with her husband, Hugh, president of the

Miners Bank. Callie was an active member of the social elite and as such knew or knew of everyone else of prominence in the city. Often she was Sabina's first choice when information about the activities and foibles of influential citizens was required, for she was an eager gatherer and dispenser of gossip. If there was anything about the Egans, or Nathaniel Dobbs and others of his Anti ilk, that could be helpful, she might well know of it.

But in a case as sensitive as this one, Sabina's cousin was likely to be more of a liability than an asset. For one thing, although Callie always promised never to reveal a confidence, she wasn't always as discreet as she should be; Sabina wouldn't dare admit to her that Amity Wellman was her client or the reason why, for fear of news of her friend's unfortunate affair with Fenton Egan leaking out. For another, Callie was greatly interested in, if not always approving of, Sabina's profession and was bound to ask too many probing questions despite Sabina having made it clear to her that professional ethics forbade her from discussing her cases.

No, she wouldn't risk questioning Callie. There were other sources of information available to her. Including another, more discreet, even more well-informed source of gossip about well-to-do San Franciscans.

It was nearly ten o'clock when Sabina arrived at Carpenter and Quincannon, Professional Detective Services. The door was locked, and when she entered with her key she found no indication that John had yet put in an appearance. This was typical of him; he seldom arrived mornings before she did. His excuses included business matters, transportation difficulties, and late-night activities that resulted in oversleeping, but she suspected that an indolent tendency and abhorrence for the mundane tasks of running a detective agency were equally responsible.

Whenever bills, accounts receivable, and the like piled up, as they always did at the end of the month, he made himself scarce for long periods. Usually, if she wasn't busy, she dealt with the paperwork herself to make sure it was all done properly instead of in his sometime haphazard fashion. But today she *was* busy. And since John had told her on Friday that he had no pressing business, she made sure before she left that there would be no shirking of his share of this month's paperwork once he finally showed up.

She spent the rest of the morning calling

on the two most trustworthy informants she relied upon. The first was the Market Street newsstand operator known as Slewfoot. The fact that he was blind, or claimed to be, was more of a useful tool than a handicap; all sorts of people told him things or said things in front of him. Both he and the second information seller, Madame Louella, who ran a Gypsy fortune-telling dodge from a storefront on Kearny Street, had a coterie of contacts that extended into the bowels of the Barbary Coast, among other parts of the city. If a hired assassin had made the attempt on the life of "a prominent woman on Telegraph Hill" last evening, one or the other would eventually ferret out the fact and put a name to the gunman.

Since she still had little useful information about Nathaniel Dobbs and the Egans, Sabina made her next stop the Commercial Street building that housed the *Morning Call.* Once known as "the washerwoman's paper," for it had been aimed primarily at the working-class Irish, it had since evolved into one of the more responsible general-readership sheets. While not editorially in favor of woman suffrage, at least it refused to lower itself to the level of the muckraking attacks in such rags as Homer Keeps' *Evening Bulletin.*

She spoke to two employees she knew, society page editor Millie Munson and old Ephraim Ballard who presided over the paper's musty, dusty morgue. From Millie she learned that the Egans, while wealthy, were not members of the city's social elite, neither having come from a moneyed background. Fenton Egan's partner, William Bradford, was largely responsible for the success of their importing firm; he had put up much of the financing to start the business, and it was his knowledge of teas and spices and their suppliers in the Orient that had made it successful. Fenton's contribution was public relations and shrewd salesmanship. If he had a penchant for extramarital affairs, Millie was unaware of it. Both he and his wife evidently kept their private lives private and had thus avoided any sort of public scandal. Ephraim, who knew a little about almost everything and everybody mentioned in the pages of the *Morning Call,* confirmed this.

Millie disliked Dobbs and his Solidarity Party on principle, being a suffrage supporter herself, but knew nothing about him or any of the other opponents to the movement that wasn't public knowledge. Neither did Ephraim. According to him, bachelor Dobbs was a "backward-leaning blowhard" and his minions "a pack of blustering rabble-rousers," and Dobbs' entire public life had been little more than a sham. His "devotion to public service" as water commissioner was the result of nepotism — his brother had been a member of the board of supervisors at the time of his appointment — and the Solidarity Party a humbug designed to provide him with unwarranted attention and a living from donations and dubious speaking engagements instead of from honest work. No public scandal had ever been attached to him, either.

It was well past the hour for luncheon when Sabina left the *Morning Call* building, and her empty stomach was demanding attention. She walked to Union Square, where she bought sausage and sauerkraut in a soft roll and a bottle of soda pop from one of the food sellers. She sat on a bench, like Little Miss Muffet on her tuffet, to eat every morsel and drink every drop. A poor and not very healthy meal, one that cousin Callie would have heartily disapproved of, but Sabina had no time for leisurely dining today.

Ross Cleghorne's Floral Delights shop, on Geary Street a short distance from Union Square, was her next stop. Mr. Cleghorne was more than just a "florist to the wealthy and influential." In many respects San Francisco was a small town as well as a growing city; many secrets were not long or easily kept, particularly those involving immoral and/or quasi-legal behavior among those in the upper strata of society. Gossip was rife, and gossip was Mr. Cleghorne's passion — to an even greater degree than it was to Callie. He collected a vast storehouse of what he called tidbits and large juicy bites, and was not above discreetly sharing it with professionals such as Sabina if he deemed doing so harmless to his business and his reputation. But he demanded a price for it, firmly if delicately: it was necessary whenever she called upon him to place an order for an expensive corsage or nosegay or one of his unique floral arrangements.

He greeted her with his usual effusive charm. No more than five feet tall and rather pear-shaped, he made up for his lack of stature by dressing in finely tailored clothing, wearing patent-leather shoes with large lifts, and combing his full head of white hair in an upswept pompadour. It was impossible, at least for Sabina, not to like the man despite his gossipmongering and his quid pro quo method of doing business.

"Ah, my dear Mrs. Carpenter," he said. "As always you brighten my day with your comely presence. It has been much too long since your last visit."

The flattery, typically overdone, was nonetheless sincere and therefore appealing. "And how have you been, Mr. Cleghorne?"

"Splendid. Business, if you'll excuse the vulgar phrase, is booming. How may I serve you? A bouquet of red and yellow roses, perhaps?"

"A small corsage would be more appropriate."

He pretended to pout, then brightened. "Ah! I have just the thing — a pair of lovely lavender-and-white cattleya orchids."

"How much are they?"

"For you, dear lady, half price. A mere ten dollars."

Sabina managed not to wince. "I'd like the answers to a few questions before I decide." This was another part of their little ritual. If he had no answers or did and refused to divulge them, she would make this known and not be held to the orchid purchase. In his own mildly corrupt way, Ross Cleghorne was an honorable man.

A bell over the door tinkled as a well-dressed woman came in. Mr. Cleghorne signaled to a clerk to attend to the customer, then said to Sabina, "Naturally. Shall we step into my office?"

His office was small, neat, and filled with potted ferns and flowering plants. Once inside with the door closed, Sabina said, "To begin with, do you know of anyone who bears a serious grudge against any of the leaders of the woman suffrage movement?"

"By 'serious,' you mean — ?"

"Serious enough to attempt to inflict harm."

"Ah. Which leader did you have in mind?"

"I would rather not say. *Do* you know of any such grudge holder?"

"The suffrage movement engenders strong emotions in its opponents, as I'm sure you know. Enemies abound on both sides. I myself must remain neutral on this and other political issues, of course, so as not to offend any of my customers." A self-serving statement if Sabina had ever heard one.

"You haven't answered my question, Mr. Cleghorne."

"Allow me to think for a moment." He tugged at his pendulous lower lip, his eyelids fluttering as he cudgeled his memory. At length he said, rather wistfully, "No, I'm sorry to say that I have no knowledge of anyone who might wish to harm a suffragist leader."

He was dying to know who that leader

was, but he didn't press her. That was another of their ground rules: she told him only so much as she felt was necessary and he wasn't to ask for more. Nor was he to include what information she gave him in his spread of gossip to others. So far as she knew, he had never broken that covenant.

"May I be of any other assistance?" he asked.

"Possibly. What can you tell me about the man who founded the Solidarity Party, Nathaniel Dobbs?"

"Very little, I'm afraid. I know who he is, of course, but he is not a customer of mine and I have never met him."

"There's no unsavory behavior attached to him, then, so far as you know."

"So far as I know. A conservative political animal, I should say." He added sagely, "Of course, there are secrets in everyone's life, some of which are quite jealously guarded."

Not in mine. Though every now and then I wish there were.

"Would that be the case with Fenton Egan, of Egan and Bradford, Tea and Spice Importers, and his wife, Prudence?"

Mr. Cleghorne brightened. "Not at all. They are also not customers of mine, I regret to say, but it is whispered that neither is a pillar of moral rectitude. What exactly is it you'd like to know about the Egans? Tidbits or large juicy bites?"

"Does that mean there are large juicy bites?"

"Indeed. Mr. Egan is said to possess a roving eye, a *very* roving eye."

"Numerous conquests?"

"Not as numerous as some of our lustier citizens', but yes, I should say he has stepped outside the bounds of marital fidelity on a number of occasions."

"With married women?"

"Married, widowed, divorced. Primarily, though not solely, those of the better class. His tastes appear to be catholic." Mr. Cleghorne chuckled. "One might say that he is a social-climbing philanderer."

"Do you know the names of his recent conquests?"

"One, perhaps, though I wouldn't care to provide it. The lady happens to be the wife of a prominent political figure."

Which meant, to Sabina's relief, that Mr. Cleghorne wasn't aware of Egan's affair with Amity. And what he didn't know he wouldn't be tempted to gossip about. "Would you say that Prudence Egan is aware of her husband's infidelities?"

"Undoubtedly she is."

"I understand she's quite a jealous

woman."

"Most women in her position are, to one extent or another."

"The sort who puts up with her husband's affairs so long as they're casual and non-threatening to her marriage."

"A difficult question to answer. I know the lady only by reputation." Mr. Cleghorne tugged his underlip into a sly little smile. "Of course, one doesn't have to passively put up with a spouse's casual affairs, does one."

"Meaning?"

"It is rumored that Mrs. Egan has indulged in a certain amount of retaliatory behavior. As a matter of fact, she is alleged to have rented a pied-à-terre in which she conducts her, shall we say, counteroffensives."

"Which implies her husband is unaware of these counter-offensives."

"Or of the pied-à-terre."

"Do you know where this trysting place is located?"

"Only that it is reputed to be here in the city."

"I don't know that it matters, but could you find out the address?"

"With a little diligent effort, perhaps. I shall try." Mr. Cleghorne rubbed his hands together briskly. "Now then. Have you any more questions, dear lady?"

"Not at the moment."

"Then I shall go and fetch that cattleya orchid corsage for you. A virtual steal at a mere ten dollars, as you'll soon see. And such a perfect complement to your ensemble and your lovely eyes."

It was too late in the day to begin interviewing the Egans and Nathaniel Dobbs. And Sabina was tired and somewhat frazzled from the long day's activities. The questions she asked and the answers and reactions she received from the trio would give her a better idea of whether or not any of them was a viable suspect. They were better asked in the morning, when she would be much more alert after a good night's sleep.

One last stop at the agency to check for messages. There were none waiting, nor had any been left for her with the Telephone Exchange. All was well with Amity, therefore; Elizabeth would have informed Sabina immediately of any new threats or difficulties with the bodyguard arrangement.

John had been in at some point, and — wonder of wonders — he had heeded her note and made significant inroads in the pile of paperwork she had set on his desk.

She felt a wash of tenderness toward him and chided herself for it because it was out of proportion to the task he'd performed. Such feelings came over her unbidden more and more often lately, rendering the (relatively minor) flaws and faults that had always nettled her in the past insignificant and excusable. She had even had a dream about him on Saturday night, a rather spicy dream in fact, the first of its kind in years. Memory of it brought warmth to her cheeks — a schoolgirl blush, for heaven's sake.

She quickly transferred the remaining bills, invoices, dossiers, and notes for reports to her desk and attacked them with vigor. But the memory of that naughty dream continued to linger in a corner of her mind.

5

QUINCANNON

From where he sat propped behind a copy of the *Argonaut,* Quincannon had an unobstructed view of both the entrance to the Hotel Grant's elegant bar parlor and the booth in which Titus Wrixton waited with the aid of a large brandy. The Seth Thomas clock above the backbar gave the time as five minutes past nine, which made the extortionist or his emissary, whichever he was, late for their appointment. This was no surprise to Quincannon. Blackmailers seldom missed an opportunity to heap additional pressure on their victims.

The banker fidgeted, looked at the clock for perhaps the dozenth time, and once more pooched out his cheeks in that habitual trick of his. Large, red-faced rodent indeed. As per their arrangement, he continued to ignore the table where Quincannon sat with his newspaper. The satchel containing the five-thousand-dollar payoff demand was on the seat next to him, one corner of it just visible to Quincannon's sharp eye.

The *Argonaut,* like all of the city's papers this month, contained considerable mention of two prominent news stories. First, rumors that gold had been discovered in the Klondike region of Yukon Territory, which if true would surely trigger a stampede to rival the California Gold Rush of '49. And second, that an American named James Connolly had won a silver medal in an event called the Triple Jump at the first modern Olympic games in Athens, Greece.

Neither of these articles, nor any others in this day's issue, held more than a modicum of Quincannon's attention; baseball and horse racing were the only two sports that interested him, and he considered men who succumbed to gold fever to be foolish. He pretended to be engrossed, however, while keeping watch on both the banker and the entrance to the bar parlor.

He took a sip of warm clam juice, his favorite tipple since he had given up alcohol, and turned a page of the *Argonaut.* Wrixton glanced again at the clock, which now read ten past nine. He drained what was left of his brandy, a sop for his nerves but not for his sour stomach; he winced noticeably and fished out his vial of dyspepsia tablets. He was in the process of chewing two or three when the man he awaited finally appeared.

The fellow's entrance into the bar parlor was slow and cautious. This was one thing that alerted Quincannon. The other was the way the man was dressed. Threadbare overcoat, slouch hat drawn low on his forehead, wool muffler wound up high inside the coat collar so that it concealed the lower part of his face. This slatternly attire might have been conspicuous if the night had retained the day's warmth; but rain clouds driven by a cold wind had darkened the sky during the late afternoon, dropping the temperature some twenty degrees by nightfall. No one except Quincannon and Wrixton paid him the slightest attention.

He paused just inside the archway to peer around before his gaze locked in on his prey. Out of the corner of one eye Quincannon watched him approach the booth. What little of the man's face was visible corroborated the banker's description of him: middle-aged, small of stature, with a hooked nose and sallow complexion. Not such-a-much at all.

Wrixton stiffened when the fellow slipped into the booth opposite him. There was a low-voiced exchange of words, after which the banker passed the satchel under the table. The hook-nosed gent opened it just long enough to determine that it contained stacks of greenbacks, closed it again, then produced a manila envelope from inside his coat and slid it across the table. Wrixton opened the envelope and furtively examined the few papers it contained — one or two but certainly not all of the indiscreet letters he had written. The rest and no doubt the most damning would remain in the black-mailer's possession until Quincannon completed his assignment.

While the two men were making their exchange, he casually folded the newspaper and laid it on the table, finished his clam juice, gathered up umbrella and derby, and strolled out into the hotel lobby. He took a position just inside the corridor that led to the elevators, where he had an oblique view of the bar entrance. His quarry would have to come out that way because there was no other exit from the bar parlor.

The wait this time was less than two minutes. When Hook-nose appeared, he went straight to the swing door that led out to New Montgomery Street. Quincannon followed twenty paces behind. A drizzle of rain had begun and the salt-tinged bay wind had the sting of a whip. It being a poor night for travel by shank's mare, Quincannon expected his man to take one of the hansom cabs at the stand in front of the Palace Hotel opposite. But this didn't happen. With the satchel clutched inside his overcoat, the fellow angled across Montgomery and turned the far corner into Jessie Street.

Quincannon reached the corner a few seconds later. He paused to peer around it, to make sure he wasn't observed, before unfurling his umbrella and turning in to Jessie himself. Hook-nose apparently had no fear of pursuit; he was hurrying ahead through the misty rain without a backward glance.

Jessie was a dark, narrow thoroughfare and something of an anomaly as the new century approached — a mostly residential street that ran for several blocks through the heart of the business district, midway between Market and Mission streets. Small, old houses and an occasional small-business establishment flanked it, fronted by tiny yards and backed by barns and sheds. The electric glow from Third Street and the now-steady drizzle made it a chasm of shadows. The darkness and the thrumming wind allowed Quincannon to quicken his pace without fear of being seen or heard.

After two blocks, his quarry made another turning, this time into a cracked cobblestone cul-de-sac called Gunpowder Alley. The name, or so Quincannon had once been told, derived from the fact that Copperhead sympathizers had stored a large quantity of explosives in one of the houses there during the War Between the States. Gunpowder Alley was even darker than Jessie Street; the frame buildings strung along its short length were shabby presences in the wet gloom. The only illumination was strips and daubs of light that leaked palely around a few drawn window curtains.

Not far from the corner, Hook-nose crossed the alley to a squat, dark structure that huddled between the back end of a saloon fronting on Jessie Street and a private residence. The squat building appeared to be a shop of some sort, its plate-glass window marked with lettering that couldn't be read at a distance. The man used a key to unlock a recessed door next to the window and disappeared inside.

As Quincannon cut across the alley, lamplight bloomed in pale fragments around the edges of a curtain that covered the store window. He ambled past, pausing in front of the glass to read the lettering: **CIGARS, PIPE TOBACCO, SUNDRIES.**

R. SONDERBERG, PROP. The curtains were made of two sections of heavy muslin; all he could discern through the folds in the middle was a slice of narrow counter. He put his ear to the cold glass. The faint whistling voice of the wind, muted here in the narrow lane, was the only sound to be heard.

He moved on. A narrow, ink-black passage separated R. Sonderberg's cigar store from the house on the far side — a low, two-story structure with a gabled roof and ancient shingles curled by the weather. The parlor window on the lower floor was a curtainless, palely lamplit rectangle; framed in it was the just discernible shape of a white-haired, shawl-draped woman in a high-backed rocking chair, either asleep or keeping a lonely watch on the street. Crowded close along the rear of store and house, paralleling Gunpowder Alley from the Jessie Street corner to its end, stood the long back wall of a warehouse, its dark windows steel shuttered. There was nothing else to see. And still nothing to hear except the wind.

A short distance beyond the house Quincannon paused to close his umbrella, the drizzle having temporarily ceased. He shook water from the fabric, then turned back the way he'd come. The elderly woman in the rocking chair hadn't moved — asleep, he decided. Lamp glow now outlined a window in the squat building that faced into the side passage; the front part of the shop was once again dark. R. Sonderberg, if that was who Hook-nose was, had evidently entered a room or rooms at the rear — living quarters, like as not.

Quincannon stopped again to listen and again detected only silence from within. He sidestepped to the door and tried the latch. Bolted. His intention then was to enter the side passage, to determine if access could be gained at the rear. What stopped him was the realization that he was no longer the only pedestrian abroad in Gunpowder Alley.

Heavy footsteps echoed hollowly from the direction of Jessie Street. Even as dark and wet as it was, he recognized almost immediately the brass-buttoned coat, helmet, and handheld dark lantern of a police patrolman. *Damn and damnation! Of all times for a blasted bluecoat to happen along on his rounds.*

Little annoyed Quincannon more than having to abort an assignment in mid-skulk, but he had no other choice here. He turned from the door, moved at an even pace toward the approaching copper. They met just beyond the joining of the saloon's back wall and the cigar store's far-side wall.

Unlike many of his brethren, the bluecoat, an Irishman of some forty years, was a gregarious sort. He stopped, forcing Quincannon to do likewise, and briefly opened the lantern's shutter so that the beam flicked over his face before saying in conversational tones, "Evening, sir. Nasty weather after a pleasant spring day, eh?"

"More coming, I expect."

"Aye. A bit of heavy rain before morning. Like as not I'll have a thorough soaking before my patrol ends."

Quincannon itched to touch his hat and move on. But the bluecoat was not done with him yet. "Don't believe I've seen you before, sir. Live in Gunpowder Alley, do you?"

"No. Visiting."

"Which resident, if you don't mind my asking?"

"R. Sonderberg, at the cigar store. Do you know him?"

"Only by sight. We've yet to meet. I've only been on this beat two weeks now, y'see. Maguire's my name, at your service."

Before Quincannon could frame a lie that would extricate him from Officer Maguire's company there came in rapid succession a brace of muffled reports. As quiet as the night was, there was no mistaking the fact that they were pistol shots and that the weapon had been fired inside the squat building.

Quincannon's reflexes were superior to the patrolman's; he was already on the run by the time the bluecoat reacted. Behind him Maguire shouted something, but he paid no heed. Another sound, a loudish thump, reached his ears as he charged past the shop's entrance. Seconds later he veered into the side passage. The narrow confines appeared deserted and there were no sounds of movement at its far end. He skidded to a halt in front of the lit window.

Vertical bars set close together prevented both access and egress. The glass inside was dirty and rain spotted, but he could make out the figure of a man sprawled supine on the floor of a cluttered room. There was no sign of anyone else in there.

The spaces between the bars were just wide enough to reach a hand through; he did that, pushing fingers against the pane. It failed to yield to the pressure.

Officer Maguire pounded up beside him, the beam from his lantern cutting jigsaw pieces out of the darkness. The bobbing light illuminated enough of the passage ahead so that Quincannon could see to where it ended at the warehouse wall. He hurried back there while Maguire had his look through the window.

Another short walkway, shrouded in gloom, stretched at right angles to the side passage like the crossbar of the letter *T.* Quincannon thumbed a lucifer alight as he stepped around behind the cigar store, shielding the flame with his other hand. That section was likewise empty except for a pair of refuse bins. There was no exit in that direction; the walkway ended in a board fence that joined the shop and warehouse walls, built so high that only a monkey could have climbed it. The match's flicker showed Quincannon the outlines of a rear door to R. Sonderberg's quarters. He tried the handle, but the heavy door was secure in its frame.

Maguire appeared, his lantern creating more dancing patterns of light and shadow. "See anyone back here?" he demanded.

"No one."

"Would that rear door be unlatched?"

"No. Bolted on the inside."

The bluecoat grunted and pushed past him to try the handle himself. While he was doing that, Quincannon struck another match in order to examine the other half of the walkway. It served the adjacent house, ending in a similarly high and unscalable board fence. The house's rear door, he soon determined, was also bolted from within.

The lantern beam again picked him out. "Come away from there, laddie. Out front with me, step lively now."

Quincannon complied. As they hurried along the passage, Maguire said, "Is it your friend Sonderberg lying shot in there?"

No friend of mine or society's, Quincannon thought. But he said only, "I couldn't be sure."

"Didn't seem to be anybody else in the room."

"No."

"Well, we'll soon find out for sure."

When they emerged from the passage, Quincannon saw that the elderly woman had left her rocking chair and was now standing stooped at the edge of her front window, peering out. One other individual had so far been alerted; a man wearing a cape and high hat and carrying a walking stick had appeared from somewhere and stood staring nearby. A gaggle of other onlookers would no doubt materialize before long.

No one had exited the cigar store through the Gunpowder Alley entrance; the recessed

77

door was still locked on the inside. Maguire grunted again. "We'll be having to break it down," he said. "Sonderberg, or whoever 'tis, may still be alive."

It took the combined weight of both of them to force the door, the bolt finally splintering free with an echoing crack. Once they were inside, Maguire flashed his lantern's beam over displays of cigars and pipe tobacco, partly filled shelves of cheap sundries, then aimed it down behind the low service counter. The shop was cramped and free of hiding places — and completely unoccupied.

The closed door to the rear quarters stood behind a pair of dusty drapes. "By the Saints!" Maguire exclaimed when he caught hold of the latch. "This one's bolted, too."

It proved no more difficult to break open than the outer door had. The furnished room behind it covered the entire rear two-thirds of the building. The man sprawled on the floor was short, sallow complexioned, and hook-nosed — Quincannon's quarry, right enough, though he no longer wore the bulky overcoat, muffler, and slouch hat that had covered him in the Hotel Grant. Blood from a pair of wounds spotted the front of his linsey-woolsey shirt; his open eyes glistened in the light from a table lamp.

Maguire went to one knee beside him, felt for a pulse. "Dead," he said unnecessarily.

Quincannon's attention was now on the otherwise empty room. It contained a handful of secondhand furniture, a blanket-covered cot, a potbellied stove that radiated heat, and a table topped with a bottle of whiskey and two empty glasses. The whole was none too tidy and none too clean.

Another pair of curtains partially concealed an alcove in the wall opposite the window. Quincannon satisfied himself that the alcove contained nothing more than a wooden icebox and larder cabinet. The only item of furniture large enough to provide a hiding place was a rickety wardrobe, but all he found when he opened it was a few articles of inexpensive clothing.

Maguire was on his feet again. He said, "I wonder what made him do it."

"Do what?"

"Shoot himself, of course." The patrolman made the sign of the cross on the breast of his tunic. "Suicide's a cardinal sin."

"Is that what you think happened, Officer?"

"Aye, and what else could it be, with all the doors and windows locked tight and no one else on the premises?"

Suicide? Faugh! Murder was what else it

could be, and murder was what it was despite the apparent circumstances.

Four things told Quincannon this beyond any doubt. Sonderberg had been shot twice in the chest, a location handgun suicides seldom chose because it necessitated holding the weapon at an awkward angle. The entry wounds were close together, indicating that both bullets had entered the heart; Sonderberg would have had neither time nor cause nor ability to pull the trigger more than once. The pistol that had fired the two rounds lay some distance away from the dead man, too far for it to have been dropped if he had died by his own hand. And the most damning evidence of all: the satchel containing the five-thousand-dollar blackmail payoff was nowhere to be seen here, nor had it been in the front part of the shop.

But Quincannon only shrugged and said nothing. Let the bluecoat believe what he liked. The dispatching of R. Sonderberg was part and parcel of the blackmail game, and that made it John Quincannon's meat.

"I'll be needing to report in straightaway," Maguire said. "The nearest call box is on Jessie two blocks distant. You'll stay here, will you, and keep out any curious citizens until I return, Mr. . . . ?"

"Quinn. That I will, Officer. On my word."

"Quinn, is it? You'll be Irish yourself, then?"

"Indeed," Quincannon lied glibly, "though of a generation once removed from the Auld Sod."

Maguire hurried out. As soon as he was alone Quincannon commenced a search of the premises. The dead man's coat and trouser pockets yielded nothing of value or interest other than an expired insurance card that confirmed his identity as Raymond Sonderberg. The pistol that had done for him was a small-caliber Colt, its chambers loaded except for the two fired rounds; it bore no identifying marks of any kind. There was no place where the payoff money might have been hidden, nor was there any sign of the remaining letters belonging to Titus Wrixton.

The bolt on the rear door was tightly drawn, the door itself sturdy in its frame; and for good measure a wooden bar set into brackets spanned its width. Sonderberg had been nothing if not security conscious, for all the good it had done him. The single window was hinged upward, the swivel latch at the bottom of the sash loosely in place around its stud fastener. Quincannon flipped the hook aside and raised the glass to peer again at the vertical bars. They were set firmly top and bottom; he was unable to budge any of them. And as close together as they were, there was no way by which anything as bulky as the satchel could have passed between them.

Sonderberg had brought the satchel inside with him; there could be no mistaking that. Whoever had shot him had made off with it; that, too, was plain enough. But how the devil could the assassin have committed the crime and then escaped from not one but two sealed rooms in the clutch of seconds that had passed between the triggering of the fatal shots and Quincannon's entry into the side passage?

6

QUINCANNON

The night's stillness was broken now by the sound of voices out front, but as yet none of the growing number of bystanders had attempted to come inside. Muttering to himself, Quincannon lowered the window and made his way out through the cigar store to stand in the broken front doorway.

The men gathered in Gunpowder Alley numbered seven or eight, drawn from nearby houses and the corner watering hole. The man in the cape and high hat was still among them. The parlor of the house next door, Quincannon noted, was now dark and the white-haired occupant had come out to stand, shawl draped and leaning on a cane, on the small front porch.

The first of a barrage of questions came from the man in the cape. "What's happened here?" he demanded.

"A police matter, sir."

"Are you a policeman? You're not dressed like one."

"No. Merely a passerby who happened to be in the company of Patrolman Maguire when the unfortunate incident occurred."

"What unfortunate incident? Has something happened to Sonderberg? I saw the two of you breaking in as I was leaving my home."

"And I heard pistol shots before that," another man said, stepping forward.

"Two of them. Was it Sonderberg who was shot?"

Quincannon admitted that it was.

"Dead?"

"Yes."

"Was it robbery? I didn't see anyone running away." He turned to the man in the cape. "Did you, Harold?"

Harold hadn't. "Who shot him, then?"

"Can't you guess?" Quincannon said.

"You mean . . . he shot himself?"

"So it would seem."

"Old Sonderberg," someone else said amid murmurs from the others. "I wouldn't have thought him the type to do himself in."

"You can't tell what goes on inside chaps like him," Harold said.

Quincannon asked, "What sort of man was he?"

"Kept to himself, never had a chummy word for anyone."

"No friends, no one who knew him well?"

"Not so far as I know. He won't be missed in the neighborhood."

The false theory of suicide had served to put an end to the men's eagerness for information about the shooting. Violence was common in the city and there was not enough spice in a self-dispatching, particularly one by an unpopular individual such as Sonderberg seemed to have been, to sustain the interest of jaded citizens. Some of the men were already moving away when Maguire returned.

The bluecoat quickly dispersed the rest. The elderly woman still stood on the porch; it was not until Gunpowder Alley was mostly deserted again that she doddered back inside the darkened house.

Quincannon asked Maguire if he knew the woman's name and whether or not she lived alone. "I couldn't tell you, lad," the patrolman said. "I've not seen her before that I can recall."

"Then she doesn't often sit in her window at night looking out."

"Not while I've been by these past two weeks. The window has always been dark."

The morgue wagon and a trio of other

bluecoats arrived shortly, accompanied by a pair of plainclothes detectives from the Hall of Justice. Fortunately, Quincannon was acquainted with neither of the dicks; they exhibited no interest in him. Nor did Maguire any longer. San Francisco's finest, a misnomer if ever there was one, found suicides and those peripherally involved to be worthy of little time or attention unless they were prominent citizens.

A misty drizzle had begun to fall again. While the minions of the law were inside with the remains of Raymond Sonderberg, Quincannon mounted a brief search for his dropped umbrella. It was nowhere to be found. One of the onlookers must have made off with it. Faugh! Thieves everywhere in this infernal city!

He drew his overcoat collar up, buttoned it at the throat, then crossed to the adjacent house. The parlor window was curtained now, no light showing around its edges. The rusty bellpull beside the door no longer worked; he rapped on the panel instead. There was no immediate response. Mayhap the old woman wanted no truck with visitors after the night's excitement or had already retired —

Neither, as it developed. Old boards creaked and a thin, quavering voice asked,

"Yes? Who's there?"

"Police officer," Quincannon lied glibly. "A few questions if I may, madam. I won't keep you long."

There was a longish pause, followed by the click of a bolt being thrown; the door squeaked open partway and the white-haired woman appeared. Stooped, still bundled in a shawl over a black dress, she carried her cane in one hand and a lit candle in the other. A cold draught set the candle flame to flickering in its ceramic holder, so that it cast a shifting motif of pale light and dark shadow over her heavily seamed face as she peered out and up at him.

"I know you," she said. "You were here before all the commotion next door."

"You spied me through your parlor window, eh? I thought as much, Mrs. . . . ?"

"Carver. Letitia Carver. Yes, I occasionally sit watching the street. A person my age sometimes feels lonesome at night. Sight of others passing by, even at a distance, can be a comfort."

"I'm sure it can," Quincannon said. "Did you happen to see anyone enter or leave the cigar store at any time tonight?"

"No, no one."

"You're certain?"

"Quite certain. What happened to Mr. Sonderberg?"

"Shot dead in his quarters."

"Oh!"

"You heard the reports, did you?"

"Two, yes. I thought they were pistol shots, but I wasn't sure. Who killed the poor man?"

"Done by his own hand, presumably. Does that surprise you?"

"At my age, young man, nothing surprises me."

"Did you know Mr. Sonderberg well?"

"Oh, no. Hardly at all. He was a surly fellow, and I have no use for the sort of goods he sold in his shop."

"Do you live here alone, Mrs. Carver?"

"Since my husband, Theron, passed on three years ago, bless his soul."

"And you've had no visitors tonight?"

She sighed wistfully. "Very few come to visit me anymore."

"Did you hear anyone moving about in the side or rear passages, before or after the pistol shots?"

"Only you and the other policemen." She sighed again, sadly this time. "Poor Mr. Sonderberg."

Poor Mr. Sonderberg, my eye, Quincannon thought. Poor Titus Wrixton, who was now bereft of ten thousand dollars as well as the rest of his ill-advised and no doubt self-incriminating letters. And poor Carpenter and Quincannon, Professional Detective Services, who were out a substantial fee if the mystery of Sonderberg's death remained unsolved and the money and blackmail evidence could not be recovered.

The old woman said in her quavering voice, "Is there anything more, young man? It's quite chilly standing here, you know."

"Nothing more."

"Then I shall bid you good night," she said, and retreated inside.

He returned to the boardwalk. R. Sonderberg's remains were in the process of being loaded into the morgue wagon. None of the policemen so much as glanced in Quincannon's direction as he crossed the alley and made his way to Jessie Street, his thoughts as dark and gloomy as the night around him.

Home was where he went, by trolley car from Market Street to his bachelor's flat on Leavenworth. He had neither reason nor inclination to remain downtown. Titus Wrixton would have long since left the Hotel Grant for his residence on Rincon Hill; a report to him could and would wait until tomorrow. Perhaps by then Quincannon would have divined at least a partial explanation for the night's strange events and some definite idea of what to do next.

His flat, once both a sanctuary and, from time to time, a place to bring willing wenches for a night or two of sport, lately seemed to have taken on a lonesome aspect. He knew the reason well enough: his consuming desire for Sabina. She was on his mind constantly when he wasn't occupied with business matters, intensely so in night's solitude. Other women no longer had any appeal for him. The carefree, randy fellow he had once been would have scoffed at such feelings, but that fellow had become little more than a memory. If ever he brought a woman here again, it would be Sabina. But he knew what her answer would be if he suggested it. No matter how she felt about him, or he about her, she was not the sort to indulge in a casual dalliance. She would agree to share his or any man's bed only if she loved him and was sure he loved her, and that meant marriage or the definite promise thereof.

Marriage. Was he ready and willing to take such a step, to share his personal as well as his professional life with a woman after so many years on his own? And if he determined that he was, was *she* ready and willing to end her long widowhood with him? The chances of her saying yes to a proposal seemed depressingly slim. Yet he couldn't go on indefinitely sparking her in the present platonic fashion; it was too blasted frustrating. A crisis point would inevitably be reached, one that could have no favorable outcome. Yet the situation had to be resolved one way or another. His bed, by Godfrey, was already too cold and lonely as it was.

He took Emily Dickinson into it tonight, not that she provided any comfort. Her poetry not only failed to move him as it usually did, it also failed to help take his mind off Sabina. Or the problem of how R. Sonderberg had been murdered and by whom, the solution to which continued to elude him — a lack of success that doubled his frustration because he prided himself on having an uncanny and unerring knack for unraveling even the knottiest of seemingly impossible conundrums.

7

SABINA

She was at her desk, once again rereading the two threatening messages Amity Wellman had entrusted to her care, when John arrived on Tuesday morning. The messages bothered her. Why would a person bent on shooting an enemy, real or imagined, write a series of warning notes in advance of the act? A misguided attempt to frighten the intended victim? Because the tormentor hadn't made up his or her mind yet to cross the line into violence? Or was there some other explanation?

John greeted her pleasantly enough, but as he folded his umbrella and shed his overcoat his smile turned upside down and became a semi-ferocious scowl. Which meant that he was in one of his dark moods, at least in part because he had spent a restless and mostly sleepless night. Smudges under his expressive brown eyes testified to that.

She waited until he was seated behind his desk before she asked, "Difficulties, John?"

"What makes you ask that?"

"The way you're scowling. You have the look of a pirate on his way to the gibbet."

"Bah."

"A business-related problem?"

"Yes, confound it. Involving a banker named Titus Wrixton who called for a consultation yesterday. He has troubles that seemed simple enough to handle, and in exchange for a generous fee I agreed to act on his behalf. Now I'm almost sorry that I did."

"What sort of troubles?"

"Of his own making that led to blackmail. And worse, as it turned out. Infuriatingly worse."

"How so?"

John didn't answer. He sat scowling, fluffing his beard, apparently having subsided into a gloomy reverie. He could be close-mouthed about his investigations at times, particularly when they weren't going well. On those occasions he tended to resent being prodded. He would confide in her eventually, in his own good time.

He changed the subject before Sabina

could. "What's that you're studying? Letters?"

"Notes. Threatening messages."

"Threatening to whom? Not you?"

"No. To a friend."

"The new client you mentioned in your note?"

"Yes."

"A wealthy one?"

"That's always the first question you ask. Financial gain isn't the only reason we're in business."

"No, but it's the primary one. Who is the client?"

"Amity Wellman."

"Ah. The woman in your Sunday bicycle club, the leader of the voting-rights folderol."

Sabina said, "*Folderol,* John?" sharply and warningly.

He paused in the act of charging his pipe, correctly read the expression on her face, and said hurriedly, "I was merely teasing. You know I support the suffrage movement —"

"It's not a subject to be teased about, now especially. Not with me, nor with any other New Woman. I'll thank you not to do it again."

"No, no, of course I won't." He looked

genuinely abashed. "Sincere apologies, my dear. I'm just not thinking clearly this morning. Those notes . . . are they genuine? Is Mrs. Wellman's life in danger?"

"Yes. She was nearly shot to death Sunday night. Do you want to hear the details?"

"Yes. Certainly."

Somewhat mollified, Sabina told him of the attempt on Amity's life, the possible suspects, and the fact that she'd hired Elizabeth Petrie to watch over her friend. She also showed him the notes. He was properly attentive but had no fresh perspective to offer. Not that she had expected him to; the entire matter was outside his experience.

"If there is anything I can do —"

"There isn't," Sabina said. "At least not now."

Since he had paid heed to her, she felt she owed him the same courtesy and made another effort to draw him out. "Are you ready to discuss the Wrixton matter now?"

He uttered a grunting sound that she took to be an affirmative. She prompted him by saying, "Infuriatingly worse than blackmail, you said. Meaning?"

"Murder. Sudden and so far inexplicable."

"Who was murdered? Not the banker?"

"No. He'll live to pay our fee; I'll see to that."

"Then who was killed?"

He related the details of his meeting with Titus Wrixton, the probable reason behind the extortion attempt, and his surveillance of last night's second blackmail payoff in the Hotel Grant's bar parlor. "The blackmailer, or the blackmailer's emissary," he went on, "is or was Raymond Sonderberg, the proprietor of a cigar store in Gunpowder Alley. He led me directly there from the hotel."

"And then?"

"He was shot to death in his locked quarters before I could confront him and recover Wrixton's letters and payoff money."

"Locked quarters?"

"Behind double-locked doors and a tightly barred window."

"It couldn't have been suicide?"

"No, though that is evidently the official verdict."

"What makes you so sure?"

John's answer to that question indicated that he was right, Raymond Sonderberg had in fact been murdered. "A puzzling series of events, to be sure," she said when he'd finished his account. "But perhaps not as mysterious as they might seem."

"What do you mean?"

"You know from experience, John, that

such mysteries generally have a relatively simple explanation."

He admitted the truth of this. "But I'm hanged if I can see it in this case."

"Well, the first question that occurs to me — was the crime planned or committed on the spur of the moment?"

"If it was planned, it was done in order to silence Sonderberg and make off with the five thousand dollars."

"By an accomplice in the blackmail scheme?"

"By the scheme's mastermind. I suspect Sonderberg was only a pawn. In any event, the second person was waiting for him in his quarters. The stove there was glowing hot and there was not enough time for Sonderberg to have stoked the fire to high heat, even if he'd built it up before leaving for the Hotel Grant."

"Then why all the mystification?" Sabina asked. "Why not simply shoot Sonderberg and slip away into the night with the loot?"

"To make murder appear to be suicide."

"That could have been accomplished without resorting to elaborate flummery of whatever sort. Locked rooms and mysterious disappearances smack of deliberate subterfuge."

"That they do. But to what purpose?"

"The obvious answer is to fool someone in close proximity at the time."

"Who? Not me, surely," John said. "No one could have known ahead of time that I would follow Sonderberg from the hotel to Gunpowder Alley. Or that I would be near enough to the shop to hear the shots and rush into the side passage."

"The bluecoat, Maguire, then. From your description of him, he's the sort who makes his rounds on a by-the-clock schedule. Still, it seems rather an intricate game just to confuse a simple patrolman."

"Exactly. *If* the whole business was planned ahead of time, and not a result of convenient or inconvenient circumstance."

"In either case, there has to be a plausible explanation. Are you absolutely certain there was no possible means of escape from the building after the shooting?"

"Front and rear entrances bolted from the inside, as I told you. The door to his living quarters likewise bolted, the only window both barred and locked. Yes, I'm certain of that much."

"Doesn't it follow, then, that if escape was impossible, the murderer was never inside the building?"

"It would," John said, "except for the missing satchel, the presence of the whiskey bottle and two glasses on the table, and the pistol that dispatched Sonderberg lying at a distance from the body. There can hardly be any doubt that both killer and victim were together inside those sealed quarters."

"The thump you heard just after the shots were fired. Can you find any significance in that?"

"None so far. It might have been a foot striking a wall — that sort of sound."

"But loud enough to carry out to Gunpowder Alley. Did you hear running steps?"

"No. No other sounds at all." John stood and began to restlessly pace the office. "The murderer's vanishing act is just as befuddling. Even if he managed to extricate himself from the building, how the devil was he able to disappear so quickly and completely? Not even a cat could have climbed those fences enclosing the rear walkway. Nor the warehouse wall, not that such a scramble would have done him any good with all its windows steel shuttered."

"Which leaves only one possible escape route."

"The rear door to Letitia Carver's house, yes. But it was bolted when I tried it and she claimed not to have had any visitors."

"She could have been lying."

John conceded that she could have been.

Sabina said, "I don't suppose there's any chance that she herself could be the culprit?"

"She's eighty if she's a day. Besides, I saw her sitting in her parlor window not two minutes before the shots were fired. That wouldn't have been enough time to have committed the deed and escaped back into her house with the satchel."

"Lying to protect the guilty party, then. A relative, perhaps. In which case the murderer was hiding in the house while you spoke to her."

"A galling possibility, if true. And still only a partial explanation." John paused, glowering, to run fingers through his beard and then fluff it again. "The crone seemed innocent enough, yet now that I consider it, there was something . . . odd about her."

"Furtive, you mean?"

"No. Her actions, her words . . . I can't quite put my finger on it."

"Why don't you have another talk with her?"

"That," he said, "is precisely what I intend to do."

8

SABINA

The Solidarity Party's headquarters was located in a somewhat shabby two-story brick building on Ellis Street. Nathaniel Dobbs, however, was not in residence this morning. The lone occupant of what a sign on the door labeled a suite — a misnomer if ever there was one, given the cramped, unkempt confines of the two rooms inside — was a tubby little man seated behind a long, cluttered worktable. He wore a green eyeshade and a pair of spectacles with lenses as thick as the bottoms of milk bottles. He seemed surprised to see a woman enter the premises, and wary and not a little scornful when he squinted at her business card. Sabina knew what he was going to say before he said it; she had heard the same tiresome twaddle dozens of times before.

"A *woman* detective? Of all things on God's earth!"

"You disapprove of women with professional credentials?"

"I do; I most certainly do," he said huffily. "A woman's place —"

"— is anywhere she chooses it to be," Sabina said with asperity. "What did you say your name was?"

"I didn't say. Josiah Pitman, though I don't see that it matters."

"It doesn't matter in the slightest. Nor do you or your outmoded opinions. When do you expect your employer?"

"Not until later today," Pitman said through pinched lips. "He has important business elsewhere this morning."

"No doubt. What time do you expect him?"

"Whenever he arrives. Why does a . . . a detective want to see him?"

"To have a private conversation."

"Concerning?"

" 'Private' means 'private.' But you may tell him that it concerns Amity Wellman."

"Amity Wellman! That —"

"Don't say it, Mr. Pitman. My response would not be at all ladylike."

The look she gave him, long and smoldering, made Pitman flush and turn his head away. Satisfied, Sabina turned on her heel and left him to stew in his vinegary juices.

Her next stop, by means of an Embarcadero trolley to China Basin, was Egan and Bradford, Tea and Spice Importers. The address turned out to be a combination office and large warehouse, with a long wharf at its backside extending out into the channel. A four-masted schooner was tied up there at present, being loaded or unloaded by a cluster of noisy stevedores.

A large sign on the warehouse wall gave the company's name in ornate, Oriental-style letters. A smaller sign at the entrance to the office repeated it and also served as an advertisement for Egan and Bradford's specialties, "the finest exotic teas and spices from the Orient and the Far East." Specific items were listed: Darjeeling and Nepalese black tea, Chinese White Hair Silver Needle tea; Sichuan pepper, Indonesian cinnamon, Moluccan nutmeg and cloves, and two spices that Sabina had never heard of, Indian garam masala and Japanese *shichimi togarashi.* "Exotic" was indeed the word for the importers' wares.

The strong mingled scents of teas and spices tickled Sabina's nostrils — a heady mixture that made her want to sneeze — when she entered an office presided over by two male clerks and a handsome young female receptionist with curled yellow hair and a thrusting bosom. The hair and the bosom, Sabina guessed, were the attributes that had gotten her her job; lack of mental acuity was evident in her eyes, her smile, and her somewhat nasal voice. One of Fenton Egan's conquests, like as not.

Sabina's luck here was no better than it had been at the Solidarity Party's "suite." The yellow-haired wench informed her that she was oh, so sorry, but Mr. Egan was not expected until early afternoon; would she like to speak to Mr. Bradford instead? Sabina briefly considered the suggestion, decided it would serve no good purpose, and declined. She also considered asking for an envelope and pen and ink, writing Amity Wellman's name on the back of one of her business cards and sealing the card into the envelope with *Mr. Fenton Egan, Private* written on the front. She decided against this, too. It would be best not to give Amity's former lover any advance warning of her profession or her purpose.

Sabina splurged on the price of a hansom cab for her visit to the Egan manse in Pacific Heights. If Prudence Egan happened not to be in residence, at least the trip would have been made in relative comfort, rather than on one of the hard seats in rattling trolleys. She wouldn't even put the fare on the expense account; call it a donation to the cause.

The views of the bay and the Golden Gate were splendid from the Heights, which, combed with the best weather in the city, made it another desirable neighborhood for the city's wealthy residents. The one drawback was that, unlike the fine homes atop Nob Hill and Telegraph Hill, those here were built more closely together along the steep hillside streets. Shouldered by neighbors on both sides and perched on the edge of a sharp drop to the street below, the Egan home had almost no landscaping to relieve its stark aspect. An architect with odd, scattered tastes had evidently designed it; it was a jumbled mixture of Italianate and Colonial Revival, with Gothic windows, exposed trusses, and a great deal of ornate scrollwork. The Egans probably considered it unique. To Sabina's eye, it was something of a monstrosity.

She asked the cabbie to wait and went to the door. A uniformed maid responded to her ring. Yes, she said, Mrs. Egan was at home. Mr. Egan, too, by any chance? No, the mister was out, and whom should she tell Madam was calling? Sabina gave her name and handed over one of her cards, saying, "Inform Mrs. Egan that I've come on behalf of the leader of Voting Rights for Women." This plainly meant nothing to the maid. She admitted Sabina and asked her to wait in the foyer.

It wasn't a long wait. In fact, Prudence Egan appeared so swiftly through an archway that she might have been conjured up out of thin air. She was in her middle thirties, slender and regal in bearing, dressed in an expensive blue tailor-made suit with a jacket bodice. Dark red hair worn in the current upswept and rolled fashion topped a somewhat narrow but not unattractive face. Eyes the color of emeralds regarded Sabina with a blend of wariness, distaste, and controlled anger.

"Mrs. Egan?"

"Yes. Come with me into the parlor."

She led the way through another archway, into a room decorated with floral wallpaper, overstuffed with rococo furnishings that included a massive sideboard, and scented with patchouli oil. She turned in the middle of the room to face Sabina. Instead of issuing an invitation to be seated, she stood with arms akimbo and studied her again with a critical eye.

At length she said, "You don't look like a detective."

"What does a detective look like?"

"Fat, rumpled individuals chewing on cigars."

"In a word, men."

"In a word, yes. Men of a certain vulgar type."

Sabina had nothing to say to that.

"Well, Mrs. Carpenter? What do you want of me?"

"As I told your maid, I've come on behalf of —"

"Amity Wellman." Prudence Egan wrapped the name in a coating of ice. "What about her?"

"She has been receiving anonymous threatening notes, three of them to date."

"Has she? I'm not surprised, given her character. But what does that have to do with me?"

"Someone, presumably the same person who wrote the notes, tried to kill her Sunday night."

A slight muscle twitch on one cheek was Prudence Egan's only visible reaction. " 'Tried' means the attempt failed, I assume," she said after a brief pause.

"It did."

"Was she injured?"

"No, fortunately."

"Or unfortunately, depending on one's point of view. I repeat, what does that have to do with me?"

Sabina said, "Mrs. Wellman was candid about her relationship with your husband."

The woman's long upper lip curled. "Including all the sordid details, no doubt."

"She also told me of your encounter with her."

"I expected as much, since you've come here. Do you think I am the one who tried to do away with her?"

"Are you?"

"No. But I don't mind saying whoever did would have done the world a favor if he'd succeeded. Amity Wellman deserves to be shot."

"Shot, Mrs. Egan?"

"Yes, shot. Is that how the attempt was made?"

Sabina nodded. "In her garden at about eight o'clock. Would you mind telling me where you were at that time?"

"I would. And so I won't. I find your insinuations insulting."

"I haven't insinuated anything. I'm merely asking questions, trying to find out who is responsible for this reign of terror against my client."

"Reign of terror. My God. You make it sound as if she is a victim of the Spanish

Inquisition. She's a whore, nothing more or less."

"A mistake in judgment doesn't make a woman a whore; it makes her human and entitled to understanding and forgiveness. Especially a woman who has done so much to further the cause of her sisters. Or don't you believe in woman suffrage?"

"I believe she has made me suffer. No woman who blatantly tries to steal my husband's affection is entitled to my forgiveness, ever."

"She had no intention of trying to steal his affection, as you put it. She entered into the affair for the same reasons many women do, loneliness, temptation, and a lapse in judgment. She loves her husband as much as you love yours."

"I doubt that."

"Mr. Egan shares in the responsibility for the affair. Surely you don't deny the fact."

"Men are weak. You ought to know, looking as you do."

"Weakness is a poor excuse for infidelity."

"I will not discuss my husband's fallibilities or my marriage with you. It is none of your business."

"It is if it involves harassment and attempted homicide," Sabina said. "Was Mr. Egan home Sunday night?"

"Now you're insinuating that Fenton might be the would-be assassin, is that it?"

"Questions, Mrs. Egan, not insinuations. In search of the truth."

"You won't find it here," Prudence Egan said coldly. "You haven't spoken to him yet, I take it?"

"Not yet."

"I suggest that you don't. He takes even less kindly than I do to scandalous and irresponsible probing into our private lives." Then, almost as an afterthought, "He has absolutely no reason to want to harm his former paramour."

"Mrs. Wellman thinks differently."

"I do not care what Mrs. Wellman thinks. Or what you think." She drew herself up, thrusting her chin forward. Anger was the dominant emotion in her now, a dark red flame to match the color of her hair. "I'll thank you to leave now. Immediately."

Sabina couldn't resist saying, "And never darken your door again, as they say in the melodramas."

"Precisely. If you do, you and your client shall hear from our attorneys."

She stalked to the archway, stood glaring imperiously as Sabina went past her, then followed her across the foyer and shut the door firmly behind her. The loud snap of the lock clicking into place struck her as deliberate, a gesture of both aggravation and finality.

9

SABINA

It was half past twelve when the cab deposited her on the corner of Market and Sansome. In view of the fact that Fenton Egan was not due at his office until early afternoon, which likely meant one-thirty or two, she treated herself to a much more satisfactory midday meal than yesterday's, dining at a nearby brasserie on shrimp salad and broiled sand dabs with melted butter. According to cousin Callie, butter was a product of the devil — bad for one's digestion and circulation as well as one's waistline. The irony in this opinion was that Callie regularly consumed gooey cakes and pastries made with a great deal of both butter and sugar, a fact she blithely ignored.

Satisfactorily fortified, Sabina once more made her way to China Basin and Egan and Bradford, Tea and Spice Importers. After this morning's session with Prudence Egan, she half-expected this visit to be another exercise in futility. But not only was she permitted an audience with Amity's ex-lover after having her card sent in to him, but he came out to the reception area to greet her personally and then usher her into his private office.

Amity had said that he was superficially charming, and so he was. He had held Sabina's hand a trifle longer than necessary, appraising her in a bold but not offensive fashion, smiling pleasantly all the while. It was plain that he found her appealing to the eye, an opinion she didn't reciprocate. He was handsome enough, she supposed, but not in the least the type of man who attracted her. Tallish, lean, with penetrating gray eyes, a considerable amount of black hair that glistened sleekly with pomade, a neatly trimmed mustache, and a small, natty imperial. His gray wool suit was expensive and immaculate, his silk cravat fastened with a not quite ostentatious ruby stickpin matched by a ring on his left pinkie. Sabina noticed that, unlike his wife, he wore no wedding ring.

His office was paneled and furnished in Philippine mahogany, the chairs covered in brightly patterned fabric. A half-smoked green-and-brown-leafed panatela burned in a copper tray on his desk, its smoke aromatic but so strong as to overwhelm the more preferable scents of tea and spices from the attached warehouse. Sabina was not fond of cigars, even the extravagant dollar variety. The only tobacco she found pleasing was the mixtures made for pipes, though the Navy Cut that John preferred was just barely tolerable.

When they were both seated, Egan said, "Well, I must say, Mrs. Carpenter, you're quite the most comely detective I have ever met."

The look in his eyes added undue emphasis to the word "comely." Sabina was used to men finding her attractive, but there were degrees of male admiration and his was clearly the sort heated by lustful thoughts. How an intelligent woman such as Amity could have been fooled enough to become involved with such a man was a puzzle. One minute in Fenton Egan's company was sufficient for Sabina to dislike and distrust him.

He waited for her response, and when she gave none he said, "Well, then. Why have you come to me?"

"For the same reasons I visited your wife at your home earlier today."

"Oh? And what would they be?"

"Your affair with Amity Wellman, to begin with."

His reaction, or rather lack of one, disappointed her. A lifted eyebrow was the only change in his demeanor; his smile didn't even flicker. "How, may I ask, did you come by that information?"

"Do you deny it?"

"I see no reason why I should. My wife knows about it. Is she the one who told you?"

"No."

"Mrs. Wellman, then. Has she retained you for some purpose?"

"An attempt was made on her life last night."

He showed no surprise at this, either. When he spoke, the mild concern in his voice had a false ring. "The devil you say. Unsuccessful, I trust?"

"Yes."

"What happened?"

"Someone fired a shot at her in her garden."

"Do you have any idea why? Or who the assailant was?"

"Not yet."

Egan picked up his cigar, puffed on it in thoughtfully. "And you think, or rather Mrs. Wellman thinks, it might have been my wife or I. Or someone hired by her or me."

"No accusations have been made, Mr. Egan."

"Your visit to my home and your presence here indicate a degree of suspicion."

"Not so. Investigators ask questions of many people for many different reasons."

"My wife denied any involvement, of course."

"Yes. Vehemently."

"A very emotional woman, Prudence."

"One might even say volatile when she perceives a threat to her marriage."

"My unfortunate dalliance with Mrs. Wellman posed no such threat."

"You wrote her a letter in which you professed to be in love with her and expressed the hope of making the relationship permanent."

Egan raised an eyebrow. "Did she show you this alleged letter?"

"No. She destroyed it."

"Of course that's what she would claim."

"So you deny having written it."

"Categorically. She made up the story about a letter to throw suspicion on me. Did you or she tell my wife about it?"

"No."

"I'm grateful for that, at least. The fact remains, Mrs. Carpenter, that I bear no grudge against Mrs. Wellman and have no earthly reason to harm her. Nor does Mrs. Egan."

"Amity says you were quite upset when she ended the affair. That you threatened to tell her husband about it."

"Nonsense," Egan said. "Another fabrication — I made no such threat. I suppose she also told you I seduced her?"

"Didn't you?"

"No indeed. In point of fact it was the other way around. I succumbed to her advances in a moment of weakness, for which I was properly chastised by myself as well as my wife."

It would be futile, Sabina thought, to point out that she knew him to be a serial philanderer; he would only have denied it. She had dealt with self-serving liars so often during the course of her career that she'd become an expert on the breed. Fenton Egan was one of the accomplished variety, his voice earnest, his eyes looking straight into hers without wavering, but he fooled her not at all.

She said, "Then you weren't upset nor the parting scene highly unpleasant when Mrs. Wellman ended the relationship."

"Not at all. Is that what she claims?" Egan shook his head. "Actually, I was relieved. I was on the verge of ending the affair myself, as a matter of fact."

"But you weren't relieved that your wife found out and confronted her."

"Well, naturally I would have preferred that Prudence never have known. I'm sorry that she found out — for her sake as well as my own."

"How did she find out?"

"I don't know. She wouldn't tell me."

Another lie? Sabina wasn't sure.

Egan tapped ash off his cigar into the copper tray, then gave a liar's sigh — the mock-sad variety. "I regret to say this, Mrs. Carpenter, but your client is a vindictive woman."

"Deserving of an attempt on her life?"

"Certainly not. No one deserves to be subjected to violence, least of all a woman. I bear her none of the ill will she apparently bears me and my wife."

"Do you mind telling me where you were the night before last?"

"Still not convinced, eh? No, I don't mind. I was at home the entire evening."

"And your wife? Was she there, too?"

"She was. Prudence and I spent the evening listening to the gramophone. A marvelous invention, don't you agree?" When Sabina didn't answer, Egan said, "I do hope you find out who is tormenting Mrs. Wellman. But it isn't Prudence and it isn't I."

There was nothing more to be gotten from Fenton Egan. Sabina rose and, keeping the irony out of her voice, thanked him for his candor. He popped up out of his chair and escorted her to the door, his hand on her elbow. Standing close with his hand on the latch, he said in a casual, off hand way, "Curiosity prompts me to ask — have you been a detective long?"

"Several years."

"You must have had many interesting experiences, the more so because of your sex. It would be quite fascinating to hear of them, I'm sure. Perhaps we could dine together one day."

The colossal conceit of the man! I'd rather dine with a wharf rat. At least they don't hide their slimy predatory ways behind a cultured façade and a rancid-butter smile.

She was tempted to put the thoughts into words, restrained herself, and said coolly, "I think not, Mr. Egan. Good day." After which she removed his hand from her arm, using two fingers as she would have in disposing of a crawling insect, and let herself out of his lair.

Josiah Pitman and two other men were busily hand-lettering signs and placards with thin brushes dipped in black paint when Sabina entered the Solidarity Party's alleged suite. The room was rife with their handiwork, propped all along one wall and stacked on tables and floor — preparations for their opposition attendance, no doubt, at Saturday evening's Voting Rights for Women benefit in Union Square. One she glanced at, a cardboard sign stapled to a length of wood resembling a fence picket, bore the slogan: **Woman Suffrage a Folly!** Another urged: **Keep the Fair Sex Out of Politics!** The others would express the same regressive sentiments.

Both men looked up at her briefly, Dobbs' tubby little assistant with lips pursed and eyes glittering behind his bottle-bottom spectacles when he recognized her; neither of them spoke. There was no need for her to ask if Nathaniel Dobbs was present. She could see him in the second of the two rooms, seated at a desk writing in a ledger with — of all implements — a quill pen with a feather several inches long.

As soon as Dobbs spied her he hopped to his feet and stepped around the desk to the open doorway. "Mrs. Carpenter, I presume?" he said stiffly. "I am Nathaniel Dobbs."

"Yes, I know. I've heard you speak."

"Indeed." He was tall and almost cadaverously spare, with a nose like a beak and a mane of hair so black it was surely dyed. In his long black frock coat, he resembled nothing so much as a giant crow with its wings folded. His voice was on the reedy side, though it deepened and became commanding when he was publicly espousing the Solidarity Party's conservative platform. "What can I do for you, my good woman?"

Sabina disliked being referred to as "my good woman" by strangers, particularly insincere strangers who made a living by treating women as second-class citizens, if not chattel. She crossed the room to where he stood, fixing him with her no-nonsense look. He backed up a step in the face of it.

"I prefer that we speak in private, Mr. Dobbs."

"Oh, ah . . . very well, if you insist."

He moved aside to let her pass into his office, then closed the door. A stack of pamphlets occupied the only other chair besides his; he removed them and with obvious reluctance invited her to sit. At his desk again, he fussed with a scattering of papers and the quill pen. When he saw Sabina looking at the pen he said, "A gift from one of my associates, it once belonged to John

121

Quincy Adams' secretary," and put it down again. He was quite ill at ease, which confirmed Amity's impression that he was uncomfortable in the presence of women. Whether he actively hated members of her sex was debatable; certainly he preferred the company as well as the dominance of his own. The fact that she was a detective as well as a woman surely added to his discomfort, though to his credit he made no comment on the fact.

At length he made a "harrumphing" sound, as if to clear his throat, and then said, "I understand you are here on a matter regarding Mrs. Amity Wellman."

"That's correct."

"I see no reason for it. That is, Mrs. Wellman and I have our differences, as I'm sure you know, but none of an, ah, troublesome nature. . . ." He harrumphed again. "Just what are you investigating that brings you to me?"

"A series of anonymous threatening notes, for one thing."

"Threatening notes? I don't understand. . . ."

"Accusing Mrs. Wellman of being a false prophet and warning her to change her ways or suffer dire consequences. The implied meaning of 'change her ways' being her vocal leadership of Voting Rights for Women."

Dobbs harrumphed, then drew himself up and said in defensive tones, "Surely you don't think *I* would write such notes?"

"Your strenuous opposition to woman's suffrage is well known, Mr. Dobbs."

"Yes, but my opposition is a matter of principle and, ah, political expediency. I hold no personal animosity toward Mrs. Wellman. Absolutely none."

"Night before last," Sabina said, "an attempt was made to shoot her at her home."

Dobbs opened his mouth, closed it, opened it again, much like a freshly caught fish. "Good heavens!"

"Fortunately, whoever fired the shot had poor aim."

"But I've heard nothing of this until now. There was no such mention in the newspapers. . . ."

"Mrs. Wellman chose not to report the incident. If you had nothing to do with the attempt on her life —"

"I did not. Certainly not."

"— then I trust you'll make no public comment about that or the written threats."

"I assure you I won't. I abhor such vulgarities. The Solidarity Party is a non-violent organization. We are —"

"Yes, I know. The Antis. Anti-progress,

anti-reform, anti–women's rights."

"That is not true," Dobbs protested. "The pejorative term 'Anti' is inaccurate. We are not against progress or reform unless it threatens the long and honorably established status quo by violating the laws of the land and the word of God as set down in the Good Book. Nor are we against the rights of women per se, only their unreasonable demands —"

"*Our* demands, Mr. Dobbs, and they're not unreasonable. I'm a suffragist, too."

"Ah, yes, well," he said, paused, and then resumed, "It is the Solidarity Party's firm belief that a woman's place is in the home, as God intended, and not in jury boxes or executive offices or involved in the making of public policy."

"In other words, to be nothing more than submissive housewives and child bearers."

"I repeat, as God intended." Another harrumph, after which he quoted oratorically and not at all aptly, " 'Wives, submit to your own husbands, as to the Lord. For the husband is head of the wife even as Christ is the head of the church, and is himself the savior of his body. Now as the church submits to Christ, so also wives should submit in everything to their husbands.' Ephesians, chapter five, verses twenty-two through twenty-four."

Sabina said cynically, "Timothy, chapter two, verses eleven and twelve."

"Eh?"

" 'Let the woman learn in silence with all subjection. But I suffer not a woman to teach, nor to usurp authority over the man, but to be in silence.' "

"Oh, ah, yes. In silence. Yes." Dobbs picked up the quill pen, dipped the nib into an open jar of India ink, found a piece of paper, and began to write on it. "Another appropriate quote, that, one I'd, ah, forgotten. I must include it in my repertoire. Timothy, chapter two, verses eleven and twelve, you said?"

Sabina got to her feet and went to the door. "I won't remain in silence, Mr. Dobbs, nor will my sisters — not now and not in the future. You and your Antis can count on that."

She went out without waiting for a response and just barely managed to restrain herself from slamming the door behind her.

10

QUINCANNON

Gunpowder Alley was no more appealing by daylight than it had been under the cloak of darkness. Heavy rain during the early-morning hours had slackened into another dreary drizzle, and the buildings encompassing the alley's short length all had a huddled appearance, bleak and sodden under the wet gray sky.

The cul-de-sac was deserted when Quincannon, dry beneath a newly purchased umbrella, turned into it from Jessie Street. Boards had been nailed across the front entrance to the cigar store and a police seal applied to forestall potential looters. At the house next door, tattered curtains now covered the parlor window.

He stood looking at the window for a few seconds, his mind jostled by memory fragments — words spoken to him by Patrolman Maguire, others by Letitia Carver.

Quickly, then, he climbed to the porch and rapped on the front door. Neither that series of knocks, nor two more, brought a response.

His resolve, sharpened now, prodded him into action. From his coat pocket he removed the set of lockpicks he had liberated from a burglar named Wandering Ned some years back, and set to work on the flimsy door lock. It yielded to his practiced ministrations in no time at all.

In the murky entryway inside he paused to listen. No sounds reached his ears save for the scurrying of a rodent in the wall and the random creaking of old, damp timbers. He called loudly, "Hello! Anyone here?" He didn't expect an answer, and none came. The house had the look and feel of desertion.

He moved through an archway into the parlor. The room was cold, decidedly musty; no fire had burned in the grate last night, nor in a long while before that, he judged. The furniture was sparse and had the worn look of discards. One arm of the rocking chair near the curtain window was broken, bent outward at an angle. The lamp on the rickety table next to it was as cold as the air, and when he shook it, its fount proved to be empty.

Glowering fiercely now, Quincannon set off on a rapid search of the premises upstairs and down. There were scattered pieces of furniture in two other rooms, including a sagging iron bedstead sans mattress in what might have been the master bedroom; the remaining rooms were empty. All the floors bore coatings of dust unmarked except by mouse droppings. A few of the wall corners were ornamentally festooned with spiderwebs.

The last of the closets he looked into, off the front entryway, proved to be the one he should have checked first. The single object it contained elicited a blistering, quadruple-jointed oath, though by this time the object's presence in the house was no surprise. The use to which it had been put was all too blasted obvious.

He left the house grumbling and growling to himself and stepped into the side passage for another examination of the barred window to Raymond Sonderberg's living quarters. From there he moved on to the cross passage at the rear, where a quick study confirmed his judgments of the night before: there was no possible exit at either end, both fences too tall and barren of handholds to be scaled.

Out front again, he embarked on a rapid

canvass of the neighborhood. He spoke to two residents of Gunpowder Alley, both of whom corroborated that the house had been untenanted for some time — four months, to be exact.

Hell and damn! He should have suspected this sooner. Officer Maguire's statement that in the two weeks he'd patrolled Gunpowder Alley the parlor window had always been dark was one clue that had slipped by him in the confused aftermath of Raymond Sonderberg's murder. Another was the claim by the woman calling herself Letitia Carver that she sometimes sat in that window at night looking out.

The burly bartender at the saloon on the Jessie Street corner provided him with one final piece of pertinent information. Sonderberg had stopped in occasionally for a glass of beer, and though he was a man who eked out a living selling tobacco and sundries and who kept mostly to himself, he had once confided a taste for Barbary Coast melodeons and variety houses.

"He didn't say so," the barman said, "but I got the idea it wasn't only entertainment he was after."

"Women?"

"Not your usual brand of soiled dove. Buck-and-wing serving girls, sure as the devil. Sonderberg had nothing to offer the performing ladies, money or otherwise."

But mayhap he did, Quincannon thought as he left the saloon. And mayhap one of those performing ladies had had something to offer him, temporarily.

In any event, the mystery surrounding Sonderberg's murder was no longer a mystery. And should not have been one as long as it had; Quincannon felt like a rattlepate amateur for allowing himself to be duped and fuddled by what was, as Sabina had suggested, a crime with an essentially simple explanation. For he knew now how and why the cigar store owner had been dispatched in his locked quarters. And he was tolerably sure of who had done the deed, if not as yet the assassin's identity — the only person, given the circumstances, it could possibly be.

Titus Wrixton was alone in his private office at the Woolworth National Bank when Quincannon arrived there shortly past noon. He was none too happy to have been kept waiting for word and grew even more agitated when he saw no sign of his satchel containing the five thousand dollars.

"Didn't you recover the money, Quincannon? Or my letters?"

"Not yet, though perhaps soon."

"You weren't able to identify the man you followed?"

"On the contrary. His name was Raymond Sonderberg, the proprietor of a cigar store in Gunpowder Alley."

"Was? Did you say was?"

"He's dead. Murdered in his quarters before I could intervene."

"Good Lord! Murdered by whom?"

"His accomplice, the actual blackmailer, who then disappeared with the money."

Wrixton made a low moaning sound, followed by a belch; he fumbled for his dyspepsia tablets. "The blackmailer . . . do you have any idea who he is?"

"A good idea, yes."

"Then why haven't you . . . ?"

"I'll answer that question after you've answered a few of mine. Why were you being blackmailed?"

". . . I told you before, I would rather not say."

"You'll tell me, sir, if you want the safe return of your money and the rest of your letters."

The banker chewed and swallowed three of the tablets, then pooched his cheeks with eyes averted.

"A woman, wasn't it?" Quincannon

prompted. "An illicit affair?"

"Oh, dear me . . ."

"Well, Mr. Wrixton?"

"You're, ah, a man of the world; surely you understand that when one reaches my age —"

"I have no interest in reasons or rationalizations, only in the facts of the matter. The woman's name, to begin with."

Wrixton hemmed and hawed and pooched some more before he finally answered in a scratchy voice, "Pauline Dupree."

"And her profession?"

"Profession? I don't see — Oh, very well. She is a stage performer and actress. Yes, and a very good one, I might add."

"I suspected as much. Where does she perform?"

"At the Gaiety Theater. But she aspires to be a serious actress one day, perhaps on the New York stage."

"Does she, now."

"I, ah, happened to be at the theater one evening two months ago and we chanced to meet —"

Quincannon waved that away. No man went to the Gaiety Theater by happenstance; intention and inclination took them there. A less than respectable "palace of art," the Gaiety specialized in raucous musical revues and bawdy melodramas — the sort of place that catered to middle-aged men such as Titus Wrixton and Raymond Sonderberg whose tastes ran to the sordidly erotic.

He asked, "You confided in her when you received the first blackmail demand?"

"Of course," Wrixton said. "She had a right to know . . ."

"Why did she have a right to know?"

"It's . . . well . . ."

"Because the missing letters were written to her, letters of a highly indiscreet nature."

". . . Yes."

"And how do you suppose the blackmailer obtained possession of them?"

"They were stolen from Miss Dupree's rooms last week, along with a small amount of jewelry. This man Sonderberg or his accomplice . . . a common sneak thief who saw an opportunity for richer gains."

Stolen? By a common sneak thief? What a credulous gent his client was! "Was it Miss Dupree's suggestion that you give in to the first demand of five thousand dollars?"

"No, it was a mutual decision. We discussed it and it seemed the most reasonable course of action at the time."

"But when the second demand arrived two days ago, you didn't tell her you'd decided to hire a detective until *after* you consulted with me."

"That's so, yes. Engaging you was something of a spur-of-the-moment decision —"

"And when you did tell her, you also explained that I would be present at the Hotel Grant last evening and that I intended to follow and confront whoever claimed the payoff money?"

"Why shouldn't I have confided in her? She —" Wrixton broke off, frowning, then once again performed his red-faced rodent imitation. "See here, Quincannon. You're not suggesting that Miss Dupree had anything to do with the extortion scheme?"

It was not yet time to answer that question. "I deal in facts, as I told you, not suggestions," Quincannon hedged. "Where are you keeping her?"

"I am not keeping her," the banker said huffily, but his averted gaze indicated that this was at best a half-truth. "Her rooms are on Stockton Street."

"Is she likely to be there or at the Gaiety at this hour?"

"I don't know. One or the other, I suppose."

"Come along with me, then, Mr. Wrixton, and we'll pay a call on the lady. I expect we'll both find it a stimulating rendezvous."

134

11

QUINCANNON

They found Pauline Dupree at the Gaiety Theater, a gaudily painted structure on Jackson near Kearny on the fringe of the Barbary Coast. A large billboard next to the entrance bore a photograph of a buxom young blond woman and an announcement in large black and gold letters that Miss Pauline Dupree was currently starring in matinee and evening performances of that "thrilling, titillating stage play" *The Wages of Sin.*

The guard on the stage door passed Wrixton and Quincannon without question, no doubt because the banker slipped him a coin when he confirmed the actress's presence. She was in her dressing room preparing for her afternoon performance. More attractive in the flesh than in her photograph, she had dark gold tresses that may or may not have been a wig and bold, smoke-hued eyes wise beyond her years. She wore a long red dress for her stage role, its bodice cut so low that the swell of her ample bosom was alluringly revealed. Rouge the same hue as the dress brightened her cheeks.

As surprised as she was to see Wrixton at this hour, it was Quincannon's entrance that caused her high color to pale a bit. But she recovered quickly, showing no other sign of recognition. "And who is this gentleman, Titus?" she asked the banker in a voice as smoky as her eyes.

"John Quincannon, the detective I told you about." The smile Wrixton bestowed upon her was fatuous as well as apologetic. "I'm sorry to trouble you, my dear, but he insisted on seeing you."

"Did he? And for what reason?"

"He wouldn't say, precisely. But he seems to have a notion that you are, ah, somehow involved in the blackmail scheme."

There was no longer any need to hold back. Quincannon said, "Not involved in it, the originator of it."

Pauline Dupree's only reaction was an arched eyebrow and a little moue of dismay. A talented actress, to be sure. But then, he'd already had ample evidence of her skills last night.

"I?" she said. "But that's ridiculous."

Quincannon's gaze had roamed the small dressing room. Revealing costumes hung on racks and an array of paints and powders and various theatrical accessories was arranged on tables. He walked over to one of the tables, picked up and brandished a long-haired white wig.

"Is this the wig you wore last night, Mrs. Carver?" he asked her.

There was no slippage of her composure this time, either. "I have no idea what you're talking about."

"Your portrayal of Letitia Carver was quite good, I admit. The wig, the shawl and black dress and cane, the stooped posture and elderly quavering voice . . . all very accomplished playacting. And of course the darkness and the candlelight concealed the fact that the old-age wrinkles were a product of cleverly applied theatrical makeup."

"And where was I supposed to have given this performance?" Pauline Dupree's eyes were cold and hard now, but her voice remained even.

"The abandoned house next to Raymond Sonderberg's cigar store in Gunpowder Alley. Before and after you murdered Sonderberg in his quarters behind the store."

"What's that?" Wrixton exclaimed in

137

shocked tones. "See here, Quincannon! An accusation of blackmail is egregious enough, but to suggest that Miss Dupree is a murderess is —"

The actress said, "Outrageous nonsense, of course. I have no idea where Gunpowder Alley is, nor do I know anyone named Raymond Sonderberg."

"Ah, but you do," Quincannon said. "Or rather did. Like Mr. Wrixton, Sonderberg was drawn to variety houses such as this one. My guess is you made his acquaintance in much the same way as you did my client, and used your no doubt considerable charms to lure him into your blackmail scheme."

"Preposterous!" Wrixton cried. "Utter rot!"

"But you never intended to share the spoils with him, did you, Miss Dupree? You wanted the entire ten thousand dollars. To finance your ambition to become a serious actress, mayhap? A trip east to New York?"

An eye flick was his only response. But it was enough to tell him that he'd guessed correctly.

"I give you credit," he went on. "You planned it all well enough in advance. You had time to make your arrangements after learning from Mr. Wrixton that I would be at the Hotel Grant last evening. You found out from Sonderberg about the abandoned house next to his cigar store; he may even have helped you gain access. Sometime yesterday evening you went there and made final preparations for your performance — applied makeup, arranged a rocking chair near the window, created the illusion of an old woman seated there during the time you were disposing of your accomplice."

"Yes? How did I do that?"

"By placing a dressmaker's dummy in the chair, covering the head with the white wig, and draping the rest with the large shawl. This morning I found the dummy where you placed it, in the foyer closet."

Wrixton made disbelieving, spluttering sounds.

The actress said, "And why would I have set such an elaborate stage?"

"To flummox me, of course. You knew from Mr. Wrixton that I would follow Sonderberg from the hotel and that I would be nearby after he arrived home with the money satchel. Your plan all along was to eliminate him once he had outlived his usefulness, and to do so by making cold-blooded murder appear to be suicide and staging an apparent vanishing act must have seemed the height of creative challenge."

The banker should have been swayed by this time, but he wasn't. His feelings for Pauline Dupree were evidently stronger than Quincannon had realized.

"My dear," he said to his paramour, "you don't have to listen to any more of this slanderous nonsense —"

"Let him finish this fiction of his, Titus. I'd like to know how he thinks I accomplished such a creative challenge."

"It wasn't difficult," Quincannon said. "So devilishly simple, in fact, it had me buffaloed for a time — something that seldom happens."

"Indeed?" she said.

"Indeed." He paused to fluff his whiskers. "Your actions from the time you set the scene in the house were these: You left the same way you'd entered, by the rear door, crossed along the walkway, and were admitted to Sonderberg's quarters through his rear door. Thus no passerby could possibly have seen you from the alley. How you explained the old crone's makeup to Sonderberg is of no real import. By then I suspect he would have believed anything you told him."

Quincannon paused, but she had nothing to say.

"You waited there, warm and dry," he

went on, "for his return from the Hotel Grant with the satchel. He locked both the entrance to the cigar store and the inside door leading to his quarters. You made haste to convince him by one means or another to let you have the satchel. Then you left him, again through the rear door, no doubt with instructions to lock and bar it behind you."

"Oh? Then how am I supposed to have killed him inside his locked quarters?"

"By slipping around into the side passage and tapping on the window, as if you'd forgotten something. When Sonderberg opened it, raising it high on its hinge, you reached through the bars, shot him twice — the first shot must not have been a fatal one, an error on your part — and then immediately dropped the pistol to the floor. Naturally he released his grip on the window as he staggered backward, and it dropped and clattered shut — the loudish thump I heard before I ran into the passage. The force of impact flipped up the loose swivel catch at the bottom of the sash. Of its own momentum the catch then flipped back down and around the stud fastener, locking the window and adding to the illusion.

"It took you no more than a few seconds, then, to run to the rear walkway and reenter the house, locking that door behind you. While the patrolman and I were responding to the gunshots, you drew the parlor drapes, removed the dressmaker's dummy from the rocking chair, donned the wig, and assumed the role of Letitia Carver. When I came knocking at the door a short while later, you could have simply ignored the summons; but you were so confident in your acting ability you decided instead to have sport with me, holding the candle you'd lit in such a position that your made-up face remained in shadow the entire time."

A few moments of silence ensued. Wrixton stood glaring at Quincannon, disbelief still plainly written on the lovesick dolt's round features. Pauline Dupree's expression was stoic, but in her eyes was a sparkle that might have been secret amusement.

"Utter bunkum," the banker said with furious indignation. "Miss Dupree is no more capable of such nefarious trickery than I am."

"Even if I were," she said, "Mr. Quincannon has absolutely no proof of his claims."

"When I find the ten thousand dollars and Mr. Wrixton's letters, which of course were never stolen, I'll have all the proof necessary. Hidden here, are they, or in your rooms?"

Again her response was not the one he'd anticipated. "You're welcome to search both," she said. Nor did the sparkle in her smoky eyes diminish; if anything, it brightened. Telling him, he realized, as plainly as if she had spoken the words, that such searches would prove futile and that he would never discover where the greenbacks were hidden no matter how long and hard he searched.

Sharp and bitter frustration goaded Quincannon now. There was no question that his deductions were correct, and he had been sure he could wring a confession from Pauline Dupree or at the very least convince Titus Wrixton of her duplicity. But he had succeeded in doing neither. They were a united front against him.

So much so that the banker had moved over to stand protectively in front of her, as if to shield her from further accusations. He said angrily, "Whatever your purpose in attempting to persecute this innocent young woman, Quincannon, I won't stand for any more of it. Consider your services terminated. If you ever dare to bother Miss Dupree or me again, you'll answer to the police and my attorneys."

Behind Wrixton as he spoke, Pauline Dupree smiled and closed one eye in an exaggerated wink.

"Winked at me!" Quincannon ranted as he stalked back and forth across the office. "Stood there bold as brass and *winked* at me! The gall of the woman! The sheer mendacity! The —"

Unflappable as usual, Sabina said, "Calm yourself, John. Remember your blood pressure."

"The devil with my blood pressure. As matters stand now she's in a position to get away with murder!"

"Of a mean no-account as mendacious as she."

"Murder nonetheless. Cold-blooded murder and blackmail, and with her idiot victim's complicity."

"Unfortunately, yes. But what can you do about it? She was right that you have no proof of her guilt."

There was no gainsaying that last statement. He muttered a frustrated oath.

"John, you know as well as I do that justice isn't always served. At least not immediately. Women like Pauline Dupree seldom go unpunished for long. Ruthlessness, greed, amorality, arrogance . . . all traits that sooner or later combine to bring about a harsh reckoning."

"Not always. And the likelihood is not enough to satisfy me. Blast Titus Wrixton, too. I don't understand the likes of him. What kind of man goes blithely on making a confounded fool of himself over a woman?"

Sabina cast a look at him, the significance of which he failed to notice. "All kinds, John. Oh, yes, all kinds."

"Bah. I earned our fee, by Godfrey, but we'll never collect it now."

"Well, we do have his retainer."

"It's not enough. I ought to take the balance out of his hide."

"But you won't. You'll consider the case closed, and take solace in the fact that once again you solved a baffling mystery. Your prowess in that regard remains unblemished."

As true as this statement was, it didn't serve to mollify Quincannon. The image of the actress's sly wink still burned in his memory. "Consider the case closed?" he said darkly. "No. Absolutely not. Mark my words, Sabina. One way or another, John Quincannon will be the one to make Pauline Dupree pay for her crimes."

12

SABINA

The doorbell at her Russian Hill flat ground out an unexpected summons early Wednesday morning, just as she finished fixing her two cats a shared plate of raw cod, their favorite meal. The animals were her pride and joy, companions that helped to combat the loneliness she sometimes felt. Adam, an Abyssinian mix, had been a stray she'd adopted, or rather who had adopted her, a little over a year ago. Eve, an all-black short-hair, had been a gift from Charles Percival Fairchild III — the strange, mysterious crackbrain who fancied himself to be the famous British detective Sherlock Holmes. The cats had taken to each other immediately and were fond of playing all sorts of endlessly entertaining feline games.

Looking down at Eve, Sabina thought of Charles the Third, who had helped, hindered, and exasperated her and John on several of their recent investigations. Charles had disappeared some three months ago, the Lord only knew where to, after the revelation of his true identity involved him and Sabina in the Plague of Thieves Affair. Like John, she was relieved that the surprisingly adept faux Sherlock was no longer around to suddenly pop up out of nowhere, often enough in outlandish disguises and with amazing bits of information and deductions, and to insinuate himself into their professional and personal lives. Yet she had to admit that she'd grown almost fond of him, now and then missing his stimulating if perplexing presence. After all, he had given her Eve and his final act before vanishing had been to literally save her life. . . .

The doorbell put an end to these thoughts. Sabina hurried downstairs. Callers at 8:00 A.M. were rare; not even John had had occasion to stop by at such an early hour. The last person who had was the nasty muckraking journalist Homer Keeps, during the Spook Lights Affair. There had been no recent case sufficiently sensational for Keeps or any of his ink-stained brethren to be bothering her, but then members of the Fourth Estate were notoriously unpredictable.

It was Amity Wellman and Elizabeth Petrie, not a reporter, who stood outside her door.

Surprised, Sabina admitted them. If their presence here hadn't been enough to tell her something unpleasant had taken place, their expressions would have. Amity appeared nervous, tense. Elizabeth's usual deceptively grandmother-like air had been replaced this morning by a stern, tight-lipped demeanor.

Elizabeth said, "I'm glad we caught you home, Sabina. I tried to call earlier, but as usual the Exchange is having problems with the telephone lines. And I wasn't sure you'd be going to the agency this morning."

"What's happened?"

"There's been another note," Amity said. "Slipped through the mail slot last night, the same as the others. Kamiko found it."

Elizabeth produced the message from the large plaid bag she carried. Although it was a knitting bag, it would also contain a small-caliber pistol that had belonged to her husband, Sabina knew.

Both the envelope and note were identical to the others in Sabina's possession, written in blue ink in a ruler-neat hand on heavy vellum paper. The words on this one read:

Fear not them which kill the body, but are not able to kill the soul, but rather fear him which is able to destroy both soul and body in hell. The wages of false prophecy is the same as the wages of sin: DEATH AND DAMNATION AWAIT YOU!

Elizabeth said, "I don't mind saying it gave me the shivers. Whoever is doing this to Mrs. Wellman is surely insane."

Sabina said nothing. She was still studying the words.

"What I don't understand," Amity said, "is why he bothered writing another note after already trying once to kill me. There doesn't seem to be any sense in that."

"No," Sabina said musingly, "there doesn't."

Elizabeth reported no other incidents, no sign of trespassers or anyone lurking in the neighborhood. She and Kamiko had made sure the house and grounds were secure before going to bed last night. Neither Amity nor her bodyguard had been able to convince the Japanese girl to reveal whatever it was she was keeping to herself, though Amity was still of the opinion that if Kamiko's secret had anything to do with the devilment she would surely have revealed it after the shooting on Sunday evening; Kamiko's loyalty and adoration were above reproach.

The girl's reticence was bothersome just the same. There didn't seem to be any good reason for her continued silence, whether her secret pertained to the threats or not. Sabina resolved to have another private talk with her.

The three left the flat together, Sabina for Carpenter and Quincannon, Professional Detective Services, and Amity and Elizabeth for the Parrot Street offices of Voting Rights for Women. As usual, John was not at the agency when Sabina arrived. Just as well this morning. The office stillness, marred only by the muted sounds of trolleys and equipage rattling by on Market Street below, allowed her to concentrate on the three threatening notes, which she spread out side by side on her desktop.

Now, with the arrival of the latest, she knew the answer to the question she'd asked herself on Tuesday morning. Why would a person deliver a series of warnings in advance of a murder attempt? He wouldn't. No one, no matter how mentally unbalanced, would have reason to write another such note *after* having tried to kill his real or imagined enemy. As Amity had pointed out, it made no sense.

Clearly, therefore, the writer of the messages and the person who had fired the shot at Amity, or had hired it done, were not the same individual.

Two people with two different motives had begun deviling Amity simultaneously, the first with quotations perhaps meant only to harass and frighten, the second with the deadliest of intentions. One of those bizarre coincidences that now and then cropped up in investigative work, as they did in other walks of life. If Sabina was right in her deduction, and she was sure she was, it doubled the problem facing her.

She continued to examine the three sheets of vellum. The commonality among the messages was obvious: all three contained quotes from the New Testament. As had the first one Amity had received and destroyed, apparently.

Sabina took her copy of the King James Bible from the desk drawer. She had read and absorbed it as a child and again as an adult after Stephen's death in an unsuccessful attempt to find solace in religion. Her recall being excellent, it didn't take her long to locate each of the three passages. "Beware of false prophets, which come to you in sheep's clothing, but inwardly they are ravening wolves" was from the book of Matthew. As was "Fear not them which kill the body, but are not able to kill the soul." The book of Revelation was the source of "And the devil that conceived them was cast in the lake of fire and brimstone."

So the note writer was not only familiar with the New Testament but a possible religious zealot as well. Nathaniel Dobbs? Yesterday he had accurately quoted a passage from Paul's Letter to the Ephesians.

That didn't necessarily make him the guilty party, of course. A great many people had the ability to quote passages from the Bible. Still, the references accusing Amity of being a false prophet doomed to death and damnation surely referred to her work on behalf of woman suffrage. . . .

Sabina's memory stirred. She leaned back in her chair, closing her eyes. It wasn't long before a small, grim smile lifted the corners of her mouth. Quickly she rose, donned her hat, coat, and muffler, and left the office, locking the door again behind her.

The main room at Solidarity Party headquarters was even more cluttered today. What appeared to be twice as many signs and placards were now propped against walls and laid out in uneven rows on the floor, and pamphlets of various sizes were stacked on tables and chairs. There was even a smattering of oversized and somewhat fuzzy daguerrotypes attached to sticks and staves, of groups of men holding aloft signs and placards similar in design and content to the ones here.

Tubby little Josiah Pitman was in conversation with an equally tubby man decked out in a checkered sack coat, striped trousers, and plug hat. The stranger had the good manners to doff his hat when Sabina entered. Pitman merely glowered at her from where he stood behind his worktable. Across the room behind them, she could see that the door to Nathaniel Dobbs' private sanctum was closed.

"Back again, are you," Pitman said in waspish tones. "Mr. Dobbs is busy. He doesn't wish to be disturbed."

"Then I won't disturb him."

Sabina crossed to the nearest wall defaced by the Anti slogans. Behind her Pitman said, "Here now, don't touch any of those."

She ignored him. Several of the signs bore the same black-lettered statements as the two she'd glanced at yesterday: **Woman Suffrage a Folly!** and **Keep the Fair Sex Out of Politics!** Another read: **Wise Men Oppose the Female Vote!** Yet another seemed to have been inspired by her book

153

of Timothy quote to Dobbs: **Suffer Not a Woman to Vote — Female Silence Is Golden!** She examined several in turn, all of which had been lettered in the same neat fashion.

The two men finished their low-toned conversation and the plug-hatted one departed. As soon as he was gone, Pitman said to Sabina, "I told you before, Mr. Dobbs does not wish to be disturbed. Kindly be on your way."

Instead of answering, she picked up one of the **Wise Men Oppose the Female Vote!** signs and went ahead to his worktable with it upraised. "Is this your handiwork, Mr. Pitman?"

"And if it is?"

"The lettering is quite well done. Very distinctive. Especially the slight curve at the tail of the vertical stroke in the capital *F.*"

He preened a little at that. "I pride myself on my penmanship."

"Perfectly straight lines, too. Ruler straight, in fact."

"Indeed."

"You compose correspondence in the same precise fashion, I imagine."

"Correspondence?"

"Letters and such."

The corners of his mouth turned down,

tightened. Now he was guarded. "No," he said. "No, I write my letters cursively. Printing them would take too much time."

"But you do print short personal notes?"

"No. I'm not in the habit of writing notes, personal or otherwise."

"What sort of stationery does the Solidarity Party use?"

". . . Stationery?"

"Heavy white vellum, perhaps?"

"No. Cotton fiber. Besides, all of our stationery is embossed."

"Why did you say 'besides'?"

No answer came to him; he shook his head instead of replying.

"Is your personal stationery heavy white vellum?" Sabina asked.

"That, madam, is none of your business."

"You're religious, aren't you." It wasn't a question.

". . . What?"

"Religious. A devout, God-fearing man."

"Well? What of it? A man who doesn't fear God and His wrath is a fool."

"Which means you're familiar with the King James Bible. Much more familiar than Mr. Dobbs, I'll warrant. The quote from Paul's Letter to the Ephesians about wives submitting to their husbands that he is fond of reciting — you supplied him with it, I'll

155

warrant."

"What if I did?" Nervousness had replaced wariness; tiny pustules of sweat dotted Pitman's forehead now. "What are you getting at? What's the idea of all these questions?"

" 'Beware of false prophets, which come to you in sheep's clothing, but inwardly they are ravening wolves.' You believe that, don't you?"

"Of course I believe it. It's the word of God —"

" 'And the devil that deceived them was cast into the lake of fire and brimstone, where the beast and the false prophet are, and shall be tormented day and night for ever and ever.' That, also?"

Pitman didn't respond. He produced a handkerchief and mopped his forehead with it.

"False prophets," Sabina said. "That's how you view women who seek and work for the right to vote. Women such as Amity Wellman."

He shook his head again, a loose, wobbling denial.

"You wrote and delivered four threatening letters to her."

"No! I did no such thing!"

"Threats of bodily harm are a felony, Mr. Pitman. Also a sin. God punishes persecutors the same as he punishes false prophets and other evildoers."

"I am not an evildoer!"

The office door opened and the gangly black-clad figure of Nathaniel Dobbs stepped into the room. "Why are you shouting, Josiah?" he demanded. Then, seeing Sabina, "Oh, ah, Mrs. Carpenter. What is going on out here?"

"I've just accused your assistant of writing those threatening letters to Amity Wellman."

Dobbs gawped at her for a few seconds, then came forward in a peculiar hopping gait with his arms flapping outward from his sides — movements that added to the fanciful illusion of a giant crow disguised as a man. "You, ah, you can't be serious," he said. His shocked disbelief wasn't feigned; he'd known nothing of Pitman's felonious activities.

"Oh, but I am. Quite serious."

"You have proof of this?"

"Unassailable proof. His handwriting. The printing on the notes is identical to that on this sign" — she waggled it for emphasis — "and the others here that he lettered."

Dobbs thrust his beak in Pitman's direction. "Josiah? What have you to say?"

The tubby little man had nothing to say, other than an incoherent sputter. A trapped look had come into his eyes as if he might be about to do something foolish and cowardly — bolt and run or perhaps crawl under the worktable and curl into a fetal position. He did neither. Instead he sank bonelessly onto his chair, covered his face with his hands.

"Look at him, Mr. Dobbs," Sabina said. "His guilt is written all over him."

"Yes . . . oh, my Lord, yes. But why? What possessed him?"

Sabina was tempted to say that what possessed Pitman was the same sort of misanthropic beliefs that possessed Dobbs and others like him, carried to the degree of criminal persecution. But she said only, "He believes Mrs. Wellman is a false prophet leading women, all women, down the path to perdition. His misguided threats were biblical in origin and intent — warnings of God's wrath as he perceives it from the New Testament."

The Anti leader's features showed anger now, not so much brought on by the nature of Pitman's crime, Sabina thought, as by a trusted comrade's betrayal and its potential damage to the Solidarity Party's platform. "Unconscionable. Outrageous. Threatening letters, attempted murder —"

Pitman's head jerked up. "No!" he said in

horrified tones. "I wrote the notes, I admit it, but I made no effort to harm the woman, I never intended to harm her."

"If you're lying, Josiah —"

"I'm not! As God is my witness, I'm not! I adhere strenuously to His commandments, all His commandments, but the sixth above all. 'Thou shalt not kill'!"

He *wasn't* lying, of that Sabina was certain. Josiah Pitman hadn't fired that pistol on Sunday evening. His motive in harassing Amity was bred of deluded religious and dogmatic fervor, nothing more. Whoever wanted her dead hated her for a different, personal reason.

Amity's life was still in danger.

13

SABINA

Before leaving the Solidarity Party's head-quarters, Sabina claimed two signs and one placard hand-lettered by Josiah Pitman as proof of his guilt. Nathaniel Dobbs made no objection. In fact, he was cooperative to a fault — either because he was a more ethical man than she had given him credit for or more likely because he feared the possibility of backlash damage to his image and that of his organization. He insisted upon making both a personal and a written apology to Amity Wellman. He also assured Sabina that he would see to it Pitman "remained available," as he put it, should Mrs. Wellman wish to press charges against him. Even if Dobbs failed to follow through on his promise, Sabina had no concerns that Pitman would attempt to flee the city or to hide somewhere within it. He was a craven individual, for one thing, and, for another, too steadfast in his beliefs. He would accept his punishment with the righteousness of a martyr.

From Ellis Street, Sabina went to the offices of Voting Rights for Women and tendered explanations to Amity and Elizabeth. Amity's reaction, aside from relief that the mystery of the threatening letters had been solved, was typical of her. She, too, took the moral high road, and for less selfish reasons than Nathaniel Dobbs. She would not press charges against Josiah Pitman, nor would she make public use of his crime in their dispute over the legal and moral rights of women. The struggle would continue as it had and as it should, on the issues alone.

The fact that her would-be assassin remained unidentified worried her, of course, but to no greater degree than it had previously. Her faith in Sabina and in Elizabeth Petrie to keep her safe remained steadfast.

When Sabina arrived at the agency, John was once again absent and there was no indication that he had come in at all today. She hoped it was because he was hard at work on the Featherstone embezzlement case, the only open one on his docket, and not pursuing his bitter vow to make Pauline Dupree pay for flummoxing him in Gunpowder Alley and at the Gaiety Theater. His failure to prove murder and extortion against her was a blow to his pride and ego. There was no telling what he might decide to do, despite Sabina's advice to do nothing at all and trust in the probability that one day the Dupree woman would be hoisted on her own petard. All too often he allowed his emotions to rule his judgment, rendering him deaf to rational appeals.

But John could take care of himself. Sabina had enough on her mind without adding him to her concerns.

There was no message from either Slewfoot or Madam Louella. If the dark-clothed figure who had fired upon Amity was a paid assassin, he was apparently not one of the usual Barbary Coast scruffs. But that didn't rule out murder for hire, particularly since the attempt had failed. No paid assassin wanted it known that he had come a cropper; he would be extra careful to keep mum. And unless he was called off for some reason, he would try again — to save face and to collect his blood money.

If such a hireling existed, there was nothing Sabina could do to identify him except to rely on her informants. The only investigative avenues open to her at this point were ones she had already explored. *Well, then,* she thought, *explore them again using differ-*

ent tactics.

Now that Nathaniel Dobbs and Josiah Pitman had been eliminated, the only two people she was aware of who had strong motives for wanting Amity dead were Fenton and Prudence Egan. Unless her friend had another personal enemy she was unwilling to admit to for some reason . . . No. She'd be a fool not to have revealed the existence of such a person at the same time she'd confessed her affair, and Amity was no fool.

Before Sabina tackled the Egans again, there was Kamiko and whatever she was hiding to be dealt with. It was improbable, now, that her secret pertained to Josiah Pitman's threatening messages. But it was also improbable that it had anything to do with the abortive attempt on her guardian's life. Some private matter, then. If Sabina could pry it out of her, it would put the bothersome issue to rest once and for all.

She rode trolley and cable cars to the Wellman home, where she found Kamiko in the side garden cutting spring flowers — camellias, irises, daffodils — and putting them into a large wicker basket. The girl was dressed today in Western clothing; her preference for the traditional kimono was confined to the interior of the house. Although the Wellmans employed a gardener, also a Japanese emigrant, Kamiko evidently spent a good deal of time there herself. Just one of the many duties she had assigned to herself was seeing to it that flowers grew year round and that as often as possible fresh-cut blooms brightened the house on a daily basis.

The girl didn't seem concerned that Sabina might have come bearing more unpleasant news. Even before she was assured that all was well with her Amity-san, she seemed to take the fact for granted. Her welcoming smile was small and brief, and her large black eyes had a curtained quality, as if focused inwardly on her thoughts. Otherwise she was her usual quiet, deferential self. She continued to cut flowers, choosing each blossom with considerable care, while they conversed.

"Do you remember our talk on Sunday evening, Kamiko, before the pistol shot?"

"Yes. I remember."

"You were about to tell me what it is you've been keeping to yourself."

"No, Mrs. Carpenter, I was not. I know nothing that will help you in your investigation."

"But you do have a secret. You admit to that, don't you?"

Kamiko said nothing, her face impassive. The shears she was using made clicking sounds in the fog-chilled afternoon.

"If you tell me what it is, I promise not to share it with Amity or anyone else."

The girl remained silent.

Sabina decided to try a different tack. "The man who wrote those threatening notes has been identified," she said. "His name is Josiah Pitman, an assistant to Nathaniel Dobbs."

Kamiko brightened. "I am glad, very glad, to hear that."

"Is the man's name familiar to you?"

"No. I have never heard it before. He will be punished?"

"Yes, though not as severely as he deserves. But he's not the person who tried to kill your guardian. Her life is still in grave danger."

Once again Kamiko was silent.

"You are afraid for her, aren't you, Kamiko?"

"Hai."

"And you would do anything possible to keep her from harm."

"Oh, yes. Anything possible. But I do not believe any harm will come to my Amity-san."

"Why do you say that?"

"She is being well protected by you and Mrs. Petrie." The girl's expression brightened then, the black eyes shining. "And Burton-san will soon be home again."

"You've had word from Mr. Wellman?"

"Yes. Last night a wire came from him. He will return from his trip on Sunday evening."

"This is only Wednesday. Much can happen in three days, you know — bad things as well as good."

"Nothing bad will happen," Kamiko said firmly. "Now, I must put these flowers in water so they will not wilt. You will excuse me, please?"

Her calm certainty was almost as exasperating as her reticence. Blind faith? Denial? Something to do with the secret she was harboring? There was simply no way of telling. The workings of the Oriental mind could sometimes be unfathomable. Not that the workings of the Caucasian mind were much better understood.

Frustrated, Sabina directed the hack driver to take her to Pacific Heights. The same uniformed maid opened the door at the Egan residence. When she recognized Sabina, her reaction was odd: eyes widening and then narrowing as if she was suddenly uneasy. She said, "Mrs. Egan is not . . .

available," and promptly shut the door in Sabina's face.

Instructions from Prudence Egan to turn Sabina away if she paid another call, probably. But then why the pause before the word "available"?

Two wasted trips, more curious behavior, and a double dose of frustration.

By this time it was nearly five o'clock, too late to make an effort to see Fenton Egan again at China Basin. She could wait here for him, but there was no guarantee that he would come straight home; for all she knew, he was one of those who joined in the nightly bacchanal along the Cocktail Route.

Chill wisps of mist curled around her as she reentered the hansom. Fog was moving rapidly over the city now, already hiding the waterfront and the bay beyond beneath a thickening cloak of gray; foghorns moaned and bleated their warnings on the bay. The kind of night ahead called for a warm bath, a hot fire, a decent meal, and bed in the company of two companionable cats.

"Russian Hill, driver," she said.

Thursday was also cold and fog laden. And mostly uneventful.

Sabina spent part of the morning at her desk, but there was nothing to keep her there beyond eleven o'clock. No messages, no leftover paperwork, no new clients or visitors of any sort. And yet again, no John. The only items of interest in the mail were two checks; she made up a deposit slip, closed up the office at eleven on the dot, and went to the Miners Bank. Her destination from there was Voting Rights for Women.

Amity was hard at work, as was Elizabeth, who had thrown herself wholeheartedly into the cause, preparing leaflets requesting donations and pledges for distribution at Saturday's benefit rally. Last night at the Wellman home had again passed without incident, Elizabeth reported. Combined with the unmasking of Josiah Pitman, this had led Amity to wonder if there might not be any more attacks on her life.

"It has been four days now," she said to Sabina. "Perhaps whoever tried to shoot me has given up or been frightened off by the miss and by your investigation."

"Perhaps. But four days is a short time. The assassin may be biding his or her time, waiting for another opportunity to catch you off guard."

"Lull before the storm," Elizabeth agreed. "A time to be extra vigilant, in my experience."

"But I can't remain under guard indefinitely. Burton will be home soon. What will I tell him?"

Since Elizabeth hadn't been told of the affair with Fenton Egan, Sabina sent her away on an errand and then took Amity aside before answering her question. "If I'm unable to identify the assailant," she said, "you may have to tell Burton the truth. A version of it, anyhow, if not a full confession."

"Oh, Lord, I pray not. It wouldn't destroy our marriage — he's a forgiving man — but it would make life difficult for a while."

Sabina refrained from stating the obvious, that Amity had no one to blame but herself. She was well aware of that and wore her regret and her shame openly, like a badge of dishonor.

Volunteers brought in baskets of hot food for a shared luncheon. Afterward Sabina felt obliged to stay on and offer her assistance. One of the things she did was help Amity prepare a version of the speech she would give at the State Woman Suffrage Convention — a sort of trial run to be presented on Saturday evening.

The fact that Susan B. Anthony would be in San Francisco in November to spearhead the fight led Sabina to suggest that this version of Amity's speech make prominent mention of Miss Anthony's impassioned comments to the judge and jury at her trial for "illegally" voting in the 1872 presidential election. "You have trampled under foot every vital principle of our government," the well-known Chicago suffragist had declaimed. "My natural rights, my civil rights, my political rights, my judicial rights, are all alike ignored." Her statements had been ignored, of course. She had been found guilty and sentenced to pay a fine of one hundred dollars, to which she had responded, "I shall never pay a dollar of your unjust penalty," and had remained steadfast on this vow. Amity also added to her speech a reminder of this shameful outcome.

The highlight of Sabina's day came as she was about to leave — a suggestion from Amity that she, too, serve as a delegate to the convention. Sabina would have been proud to wear one of the official campaign badges — a silky golden-yellow rectangle fringed at both ends, California gold being the adopted color of the suffrage campaigns in the state. The demands of her work, however, limited her free time, and she might be deeply involved in a case come

November. She declined with sincere re-
grets.

14

QUINCANNON

Sabina may have been right that women of Pauline Dupree's ilk would one day suffer a harsh reckoning, but someday was not soon enough for him. Nor was the prospect that not he but another servant of the law would have the satisfaction of bringing her to her just desserts. The woman had made a fool of him, placed a spot of tarnish on his otherwise exemplary record as a private investigator; he would not rest until the spot had been removed.

Without telling Sabina of his intentions, he had set out immediately to find ways and means. Searching the actress's living quarters or her theater dressing room would be a futile undertaking; the ten thousand dollars she had extorted from Titus Wrixton would be well and cleverly hidden, perhaps in a safe-deposit box in a bank other than Woolworth National. Bracing her again would be just as futile. She was immune to threats. Neither tricks nor bluffs would work on her, either. What he needed in order to devise a method of ending her criminal career was more information about her and her activities.

It took him the better part of three days to compile a sketchy but useful dossier. He accomplished this by checking public records, bribing a minor official of his acquaintance in the police department's records department, and putting the word out to Ezra Bluefield, who still knew everything that went on in the Barbary Coast even though he no longer owned the infamous Terrific Street deadfall called the Scarlet Lady, and to others in the coterie of informants he had cultivated; by dispatching Chauncey Philpotts, one of the agency's part-time employees, to cautiously interview the other performers and staff of the Gaiety Theater; and, once Quincannon learned that his quarry had spent several months performing in Sacramento before moving to San Francisco, by sending a wire requesting information to a fellow private detective in the capital city.

Pauline Dupree's origins were hazy, though she had apparently first seen the light of day in the Sierra foothills town of

Sonora some twenty-five years ago. She had begun traveling with a motley group of small-time actors while in her mid-teens, left them to join another thespian group in Virginia City, Nevada, and moved on from there to Sacramento, where she had been arrested and fined for performing a one-woman show that was deemed lewd and lascivious. After that she had made her way to San Francisco and the Gaiety, where she had been employed for the past three years.

La Dupree had made profitable use of her time here, consorting with — and no doubt finding ways to fleece — several men of both high and low repute. Titus Wrixton was not the only prominent individual to succumb to her charms; while keeping him on her string and at the same time conspiring with Raymond Sonderberg, she had also been keeping company with a San Joaquin Delta rancher and businessman named Noah Rideout. An amazingly amoral and ruthless woman, Pauline Dupree. And one, Quincannon reflected, with a remarkable amount of physical stamina.

Rideout, it developed, was a very wealthy gent of fifty-seven years who had had two wives and at least one known mistress and who spent a considerable amount of his time in San Francisco as well as in Sacramento and Stockton. He owned much of the rich Schyler Island croplands, having forced several small farmers to sell their land to him at low prices, and earned the enmity of others by a tireless campaign to build more levee roads as a means of flood control. He had also been a leader in the legal battle against hydraulic gold mining in the Mother Lode, the dumping of billions of cubic yards of yellow slickens that had clogged rivers and sloughs and destroyed farmland. The California Debris Commission Act, passed in 1893, had made the discharge of debris into the rivers illegal and virtually put the hydraulickers known as the Little Giants out of business.

An even riper plum for the picking, Noah Rideout. Surely Dupree would have taken financial advantage of his attraction to her. Extortion of the same sort as she had perpetrated on Wrixton, using another confederate as the go-between? Either that or some equally devious means of separating Rideout from a large amount of cash.

A plainspoken interview with Rideout was indicated, once the rancher's present whereabouts had been determined. Meanwhile Quincannon decided to have another talk with Titus Wrixton. Not an easy proposition considering that the banker remained completely under the actress's spell and refused to see him. Refused to pay the balance of the agency's fee as well, which Quincannon had communicated by means of a brief note delivered by messenger — a default that rankled him almost as much as the Dupree woman's duplicity.

On Friday morning he hied himself to the Woolworth National Bank. The fact that Wrixton once again refused an audience deterred him not at all. A casual question of one of the tellers, while changing a fifty-dollar greenback, brought him the information that Wrixton took his luncheon break from twelve until one-thirty. At a quarter to twelve Quincannon took up a position outside the bank. The decision to be early was a wise one, for Wrixton emerged not more than three minutes later.

The banker was alone and, from the look of him, in a state of some distress. His shoulders were slumped, his gait burdensome, his florid features hangdog. Bracing him on the crowded street wouldn't do; a measure of privacy was necessary for the conversation Quincannon intended to have with him. He might be on his way to meet someone. If so, then the best place for contact to be made was in the reception area of whichever restaurant he entered.

Except that where Wrixton was bound was not a restaurant. Rather, it was the Reception Saloon at Sutter and Karny, the traditional first stop on the businessman's nightly eating and drinking revel along the Cocktail Route. Quincannon was only a few yards behind him, and when he himself entered he saw the banker head straight for an empty section at the far end of the long, polished mahogany bar and there stand, or rather hunch, with his elbows propped on the gleaming bar top. He waited until the banker had been served a large pony of brandy, then sauntered ahead and bellied up next to him.

"Drinking your lunch today, Mr. Wrixton?"

The banker lifted his nose from the brandy, blinked in recognition, and then glowered. It wasn't much of a glower, being tempered by a despair that was even more evident at close quarters.

"I told you before, Quincannon, you'll not get another penny from me. Not only did you grievously defame Miss Dupree, you've failed to find and return my letters as you promised to do. Dereliction of duty on all fronts."

A slanderous and inaccurate comment, on which Quincannon forbore comment.

"Money is not the reason I'm here. Not directly, that is."

"Damn your eyes, this new development is all your fault."

"What new development? Don't tell me your paramour has broken off relations with you?"

Wrixton cast furtive glances along and behind the bar. He said *sotto voce,* "For God's sake, keep your voice down. I am known in here."

"We can move over to a table if you like."

"No. I won't go to a table and I won't stand here with you. Leave me be. I have nothing to say to you."

"But I have some things to say to you."

The habitual act of cheek pooching, which Wrixton indulged in just then, had a convulsive aspect today. He drank deeply from the snifter of brandy.

"They concern Pauline Dupree," Quincannon said.

"I refuse to listen to any more of your scurrilous lies."

"Facts, sir, not lies. The plain unvarnished truth."

"If you don't leave, I'll tell the bartender you're harassing me."

"Then I'll tell him about you and Miss Dupree."

"You wouldn't dare —"

"Wouldn't I?"

For a clutch of seconds Wrixton brooded into his brandy; then he abruptly lifted the glass again. The swallow he took this time was substantial enough to make him choke and start him coughing. His round face flamed scarlet; globules of sweat popped out on his forehead. When he had his breathing under control he produced a linen handkerchief and swabbed his mouth and face with it, pooching his cheeks as he did so.

Quincannon said, "Do you know a man named Noah Rideout?"

"Who? No."

"Wealthy farmer on Schyler Island in the San Joaquin Delta. His business interests often bring him to San Francisco."

"That is no concern of mine."

"Ah, but it is. You and he share common interests, and have for some time. The Gaiety Theater for one. Pauline Dupree for another."

A dark flush moved up out of Wrixton's celluloid collar. "Another of your damned lies. Paula has never been unfaithful to me."

That last statement might have been sardonically amusing if it weren't so pathetic. "I have it on good authority that she has, often. With Noah Rideout and others."

"I don't believe you."

"Not only that," Quincannon said, stretching the truth as he knew it, "but it's likely she arranged to extort a large sum of money from Rideout, just as she did from you."

"More of your slanderous poppycock."

"On the contrary. Your devotion to the lady is completely unwarranted. She is, in fact, no lady, but exactly what I accused her of being — a schemer, an extortionist, and a cold-blooded murderess."

Wrixton half-turned, drawing his arm back as if he intended to take a swing at Quincannon — a serious error in judgment had he gone through with it. But he didn't. His anger faded as quickly as it had appeared; his shoulders drooping again, he leaned heavily against the beveled edge of the bar.

"Go away," he said in a dull voice. "Just go away and let me suffer in peace."

"Suffer, Mr. Wrixton? *Did* she break off relations?"

Silence. Quincannon repeated the question, with greater emphasis. This time it elicited a reply.

"In the worst possible way. She's leaving."

"Leaving? You mean leaving the city?"

"Driven to it by you and your disgusting accusations."

Damn and damnation! "Bound for the East, I suppose?"

"Yes. To realize her ambition to perform on the New York stage. I tried to talk her out of it, but she . . ." Wrixton wagged his head. "She is a very determined woman."

"Cunning" and "ruthless" were better descriptive adjectives. "I take it she hasn't already gone. How soon?"

"Tonight. On one of the Sacramento packets."

Now that was interesting. If Dupree was in fact bound for New York, she would have to make transcontinental train connections in Sacramento. Why, then, would she take an overnight packet to the capital city when the trip could be made much more quickly via ferry to Oakland and a Southern Pacific train from there?

"Did you ask her why she is traveling by steamer?"

"No, and she didn't say."

"But you're certain that's her mode of transportation?"

"I saw the steamer tickets in her room last night."

"Which packet or line?"

"I didn't look at them that closely. What does it matter?"

It mattered a great deal to Quincannon,

though he didn't say so. "Are you planning to see her off?"

"There's no point in it," Wrixton said morosely. "It was difficult enough saying good-bye to her last evening. She promised to write, and to allow me to visit her in New York once she becomes established, but it's such a long way, three thousand miles. . . ." The banker wagged his head again, sighed, performed his rodent imitation, then emptied the pony and signaled to the aproned, mustached bartender to refill it. He didn't seem to notice when Quincannon took his leave.

Several steamers departed San Francisco for Sacramento every day and evening. Some were primarily cargo boats, dropping off and picking up goods at numerous small wharves and brush landings in the Sacramento River Delta; others were mainly passenger carriers, offering private staterooms, good food, and other amenities, and made only a few stops en route. Most of the passenger packets left early in the morning, but there were three that departed at 6:00 P.M. daily for overnight runs to the capital city.

Quincannon made the rounds of the companies that operated the night boats, starting with Southern Pacific. The story he had concocted was well designed: his sister, Miss Pauline Dupree, had wired him that she had booked passage for Sacramento this evening and asked him to join her, but she had neglected to state the name of the packet. The simplicity of the fabrication and his gentlemanly dress and demeanor brought a respectful response from the clerk he spoke to. What it didn't bring was the answer he sought. Pauline Dupree was not on the passenger list for the SP's evening stern-wheeler.

He was told the same at the offices of Sacramento Transportation. And again at the Union Transportation Company.

Had Titus Wrixton lied to him or gotten the day or time of her departure wrong? Were the steamer tickets he'd seen in her room a ruse of some kind? None of those possibilities seemed likely. Wrixton had been too swaddled in gloom to have mistaken the day or time or made the effort to concoct a lie, and the woman had no conceivable reason to have bought tickets she had no intention of using.

A thought struck Quincannon as he was leaving the Union Transportation offices. What if Pauline Dupree had deliberately misled Wrixton as to her destination? Noah Rideout's Schyler Island holdings were in the San Joaquin Delta, and if memory served there was a steamer landing, Kennett's Crossing, not far away. Could she be planning a visit to Rideout's farm before proceeding on to Sacramento?

Quincannon went back inside and commenced another consultation with the UT clerk by stating that his sister was somewhat scatterbrained and might have decided at the last minute to travel first to Stockton and then to the capital city, instead of the other way around. Was Miss Dupree booked on their Stockton packet this evening? Yes, she was — a stateroom on the *Captain Weber,* the line's fastest stern-wheeler. And yes, the *Captain Weber* serviced Kennett's Crossing when a request was made.

One stateroom was left unbooked for tonight, or it was until Quincannon reserved it under the name James Flint. He did so without hesitation. He had no pressing business to keep him in the city over the next three days, and Sabina was unlikely to require his assistance on the Amity Wellman investigation. He was free to pursue Pauline Dupree and his lovelorn fool of a client's ten thousand dollars and batch of missing letters. If the actress was on her way to meet Noah Rideout, Quincannon would put himself in a position to end her criminal

career on Schyler Island, one way or another.

15

QUINCANNON

He arrived at the UT wharf at five o'clock. The early arrival was deliberate, in the hope that he would already be on board when Pauline Dupree appeared. He would have come even earlier, but it had been necessary to return to his flat on Leavenworth to pack his cowhide valise and then to stop in at the offices of Carpenter and Quincannon, Professional Detective Services. Sabina hadn't been there, which was probably just as well, since it allowed him to avoid lengthy explanations and a probable reprimand. He'd written her a short message:

In haste —
Bound for San Joaquin Delta aboard night boat this evening, on the trail of P. Dupree. May be away for several days. Will wire details and developments if so.
Have gathered sufficient evidence to

prove Featherstone guilty of embezzlement. No time to deliver report to client as promised. Regret task is now yours. Will make it up to you upon return.

Your Devoted Servant,
John

The *Captain Weber* was a fairly new sternwheeler, having been built in 1892. One hundred and seventy-five feet in length, with a modern, high-revolution compound engine, she had slim, graceful hull lines and three decks, the uppermost weather deck containing the pilothouse and officers' quarters. Despite being well-appointed and the fastest boat on the Stockton run, she carried fewer passengers on the average than the other packets. The reason for this was Mrs. Sarah Gillis, who had inherited the Union Transportation Company after her husband's death and who was an outspoken leader of the Stockton local of the W.C.T.U. The *Captain Weber* and her sister boat, the *Dauntless,* were the only two dry packets on either river. Either Pauline Dupree wasn't aware of this or alcohol was not one of her many vices.

Freight wagons and baggage vans clogged the wharfside, joining with the deep-throated bellows of foghorns to create a constant din. Burly roustabouts unloaded sacks and boxes of freight, passenger luggage, and steamer trunks and trundled them up the aft gangplank. A smattering of travelers had already boarded, and a well-dressed gentleman and a handsome woman in a large hat preceded Quincannon up the forward gangplank to the steerage and cargo deck. He wondered idly if they were married or if they might be about to indulge in a clandestine extramarital or premarital dalliance. The night boats to Sacramento and Stockton had a reputation among the city's upper class as discreet floating bagnios.

A few of the early arrivals were clustered along the deck railings, watching the loading process — a scant few, for the evening was cold, the bay shrouded in thick, wet fog. This worked to Quincannon's advantage, allowing him to wear his chesterfield, a wool muffler drawn up tightly over the lower half of his face, and a woolen cap pulled down over his forehead. Anyone who knew him by sight, Pauline Dupree included, would have to stand close to recognize him. Valise in hand, he ascended to the deckhouse, where the Social Hall and the staterooms were located, and took up a position among the watchers at the hammock-netted rail there that allowed him a clear view of the gangplank.

More passengers began to arrive on foot and by hansom. Small merchants, miners, sun-weathered farmers and farmhands, and coolie-hatted Chinese remained on the steerage deck; the more affluent continued on up the stairway to the deckhouse. It was five-thirty by Quincannon's stem-winder when a hansom delivered Pauline Dupree.

He watched her alight — she was alone — and make her approach. Dusk was descending; electric lamps had been lit along the wharf, lanterns on the gangplank. He had a clear view of her as she mounted, one gloved hand on the railing, the other clutching a large neutral-color carpetbag that looked to be moderately heavy. She was regally dressed in a heavy wool hooded cape of red and gold, high-button calfskin shoes, and a red ostrich-plumed hat atop her dark gold hair.

She allowed one of the deckhands to help her aboard but not to relieve her of the carpetbag, then climbed the staircase looking neither left nor right and proceeded into the tunnellike hallway that bisected the deckhouse lengthwise, where the entrances to starboard and larboard staterooms faced each other across the wide plank deck.

Quincannon followed, waiting a few seconds to give her time to present herself to the cabin steward. Then he entered slowly, in time to watch the steward show her to her stateroom, the forward most in the starboard row.

When she was inside with the louvered door closed and the steward returned, he claimed his own stateroom near the aft larboard end.

It was well appointed, the upholstery red plush, the paneling of tongue-and-groove pine, brass lamps polished to a bright sheen. None of this made an impression; he had traveled the far more opulently furnished Mississippi River steamers during his years in Baltimore. He stayed just long enough to deposit his valise and shutter the window, locking the door behind him with the key provided by the steward. Outside again, he made his way forward to a place at the rail where he could keep an eye on the passage between the deckhouse exit and the Social Hall.

Pauline Dupree did not join the handful of other passengers on deck when the gangplank was raised at exactly six o'clock. The *Captain Weber*'s buckets astern immediately began to churn the water in a steady rhythm; her whistle, which had been shrilling an all-aboard and all-visitors-ashore warning, altered cadence to become a steerage signal for the pilot. Competing whistles sounded and bells clanged elsewhere along the waterfront as the other night packets commenced backing down from their berths. There was a period of controlled chaos as the boats, flags flying from their jackstaffs and from their verge staffs astern, maneuvered for right-of-way in the heavy mist. Columns of smoke from their stacks joined with the fog to turn the evening sky a sooty gray-black.

When the *Captain Weber* was well clear of the wharves and the other packets, her speed increased steadily. As she passed near Fort Alcatraz, where a garrison of soldiers had stood ready to repel attacks by Rebel privateers during the Civil War (none such had taken place), Quincannon crossed through the passage to the starboard side. Cautiously he approached the window of Pauline Dupree's stateroom. It was shuttered, but thin strips of lamplight leaked palely through the downturned slats.

Accompanied by the throb of foghorns, the steamer progressed north into San Pablo Bay. From that point their course, and that of the other boats, would be east into the narrow Carquinez Strait and southeast past Cripp's Island to the confluence of the Sacramento and San Joaquin rivers; there they would swing south and proceed along a circuitous route among the myriad delta islands to their final destinations.

The icy evening wind blowing across the bay eventually drove him into the Social Hall. This was where coffee, tea, and other non-alcoholic beverages could be purchased, gentlemen passengers smoked pre- and post-prandial cigars and engaged in friendly games of poker, chess, and checkers, and ladies and couples played bridge or whist. There was even entertainment of a sort, which tonight consisted of a gaudily outfitted gent strumming industriously on a banjo. Quincannon warmed himself with two cups of hot clam juice. After the second cup, he went out on deck and again reconnoitered her stateroom windows. The faint light glow through the slats attested to the fact that the actress was still closeted inside. And likely intended to remain there.

He'd had faint hopes, now gone, that she would crave company in the Social Hall and be away long enough for him to surreptitiously pick the lock on her stateroom door and conduct a quick search. It was unlikely that she would have risked carrying ten thousand dollars in cash on a crowded riverboat; she was brazen, but no fool.

Chances were she had taken steps to safeguard it. Sent the cash, carefully packed, on ahead of her by railroad express to New York, if that was in fact her final destination. Or opened an account at a San Francisco bank other than the Woolworth National and arranged to have the funds transferred to an eastern bank. But if he'd been able to gain access he might have discovered Titus Wrixton's letters, if Dupree had chosen to keep them, or other telltale evidence among her possessions.

Quincannon climbed to the weather deck and entered the purser's cubicle. "What time do we reach Kennett's Crossing?" he asked.

"Shortly before midnight, sir."

"Is a stop scheduled there tonight?"

The thin, bewhiskered purser consulted his passenger manifest. "Yes," he said, "a request has been made." That was all he'd say, but Quincannon thought it was enough to confirm his suspicions.

In the lamplit deckhouse tunnel, Negro and Chinese waiters were busily setting up long, linen-covered tables. Dinner was served here, as on all the river packets, since none had space for separate dining rooms. Quincannon had no intention of eating with the other passengers, lest Pauline Dupree put in an appearance while he was doing so. But neither did he intend to skip the meal; he'd had no lunch and already his innards were complaining. He tipped the dining steward a silver dollar for the privilege of having his meal — a dozen raw oysters on the half shell, venison stew, fresh vegetables — delivered to his stateroom.

The food was delivered shortly after the mealtime hubbub began. He ate slowly, then sat planning strategy through a pipeful of Navy Cut. Given the late hour of their arrival at Kennett's Crossing, and if Dupree was in fact bound for Noah Rideout's Schyler Island farm, it seemed probable that she would be met at the landing by Rideout or one of his minions. There was an inn there, but it was as primitive as the rest of the little backwater hamlet — not the sort of place a woman like her would find comfortable even for part of a night if it could be avoided.

What he would do then, Quincannon thought, was follow her off the *Captain Weber* at a distance, taking care to avoid being seen, and put up at Kennett's Inn himself. In the morning he would get directions to Rideout's property, rent a horse, and ride there. The element of surprise and whatever cunning was necessary should have the desired results. Assuming, of course, that Noah Rideout was not the same sort of obdurate, lovesick ignoramus as his Titus Wrixton. And judging by the landowner's reputation, he was susceptible to but not blinded by feminine charms.

Once the dining period ended, silence, broken only by the rhythmic chunking of the stern buckets, descended on the packet. Quincannon read for a while in the book he'd brought along, Ralph Waldo Emerson's splendid *May Day and Other Poems,* then dozed until his trained mind brought him alert at eleven. Twenty-five minutes later by his stem-winder, he donned chesterfield, scarf, and cap and then, carrying his valise, went out to the forward deckhouse observation area.

He stood in the shadows along the rail, loaded and fired his pipe. The packet was on her winding course among the San Joaquin Delta islands now, the weather here mostly clear except for patches of ground mist, the wind light and not as cold.

His wait lasted some fifteen minutes. During that time he expected Pauline Dupree to emerge from the deckhouse with her carpetbag in hand, but when they traversed a bight in the river and Kennett's Crossing's lantern-lit landing appeared ahead, she had yet to put in an appearance. Nor did she emerge as the *Captain Weber* slowed and the pilot began whistling their arrival. Or when the packet nosed up to the rickety dock. Or when deckhands swiftly lowered the gangplank.

No one disembarked.

But someone boarded — a lone male. After which the gangplank was quickly raised and the *Captain Weber* swung out again into the channel.

Nonplussed, Quincannon watched the new passenger climb the stairs to the deckhouse, a small possibles bag looped over his shoulder. There was enough lantern light and pale moonlight to make out the features of a man no older than thirty-five dressed in a long buffalo-skin coat. The man passed him without a glance, went into the deckhouse.

On impulse Quincannon followed, peering around the corner in time to see the newcomer knock on the door of Pauline Dupree's stateroom. It opened immediately and the man disappeared inside.

Hell, damn, and blast!

Who was he? Not Noah Rideout, who was twenty years older and sufficiently wealthy to encase himself in clothing of a much better quality. Another of Pauline Dupree's paramours or pawns? If so, it seemed probable that he had some connection with her plans and that those plans concerned Rideout; the late-night boarding at Kennett's Crossing augered against any other explanation.

Grumbling and glowering, Quincannon returned to the observation area to fetch his valise. He took it into his stateroom, then almost but not quite closed the door, leaving a crack through which he could look out into the tunnel. He stood watch there for the better part of half an hour. Buffalo Coat had evidently been invited to spend the rest of the night with the promiscuous, duplicitous Miss Dupree.

It now appeared that she intended to travel all the way to Stockton. To meet Noah Rideout there or for some other purpose? And just who the devil was the fellow who'd boarded at Kennett's Crossing?

16

SABINA

Her Friday began with a telephone call from Cornelius Sutton, the head of Sutton Securities Incorporated and the man who had hired John to investigate the suspected embezzlement by Robert Featherstone, the financial management firm's chief accountant. The crotchety old gentleman (John's description) was indeed crotchety this morning; he had been promised a report by close of business yesterday and had not received it. He became even more irate when Sabina informed him that John was not in the office and she had no idea where he was or when he would make himself available. The poor connection, another problem the Telephone Exchange was plagued with lately, saved her from having to listen and respond to a series of additional grumbles. She said, or rather shouted, that Mr. Quincannon would be in touch as soon as possible and then broke the connection.

John had been to the office sometime yesterday, evidently with the intention of preparing his report on Featherstone for delivery to Mr. Sutton. Sabina discovered this by checking his desk. The ink-stained blotter had been empty when she left for the bank and Voting Rights for Women; the Featherstone file now sat in the middle of it. She opened it and read through the contents. The evidence it contained, as his note had indicated, seemed mostly complete, but whether or not it was damning enough to satisfy their client she couldn't be certain.

Why hadn't John delivered it? Or at least contacted Mr. Sutton? It wasn't like him to shirk his duties, especially when a substantial compensation was to be had. Something must have happened to deter him. The thought that it might be something perilous was disturbing and she quickly banished it.

She debated delivering the file to Mr. Sutton herself. No, not unless it was absolutely necessary. All she knew of his investigation was what was in the file, John having considered it routine and not worth discussing in detail. If it wasn't complete enough to satisfy the crotchety old gentleman, there was little she could do to appease him. Better to wait and hope that John would finally put in an appearance this morning and ease her mind on all counts.

But he didn't.

Eleven o'clock came and went. Nothing disturbed the empty silence in the office except for the arrival of the day's mail, which consisted of circulars and the latest issue of the *Police Gazette.* Where was he, for heaven's sake?

Eleven-forty-five. On most Fridays, she lunched with Callie at one of the better downtown restaurants; they had an appointment to meet today at the Sun Dial. Callie would be on her way there now, so it was too late to call it off. And if Sabina didn't show up, Callie, who constantly worried about her cousin's involvement in what she considered a hazardous profession, would think the worst. In which case there was no telling what she might do.

Reluctantly, Sabina kept the date. Callie was her usual effusive self, chatting on about all sorts of things, including Sabina's budding romance with John, for Callie would have liked nothing better than to see her married again. Sabina had become adept at sidetracking this well-meaning prying and did so again today. But the rambling comments and questions, and Callie's fondness for sweets, made the lunch a lengthy chore. It was two o'clock before Sabina could extricate herself and shortly past two-thirty before she arrived back at the agency.

The door was still locked, but John had been there in her absence. He hadn't stayed long, however, and he hadn't taken the Featherstone file with him when he left. Instead he'd transferred it from his desk to hers and placed a note in his crabbed hand on top of it.

The note irritated and puzzled her. *On the trail of P. Dupree.* So that was what had been occupying John's time since Tuesday, just as she'd suspected. But what did "on the trail" mean, exactly? And why was he taking a night boat to the San Joaquin Delta, of all places? If the actress had suddenly decided to leave San Francisco with her ill-gotten gains in order to pursue her New York stage ambitions, the logical route would have been by steamer to Sacramento and thence a transcontinental train. There must be some reason she was bound for the delta, assuming that was why John was bound there. *May be away for several days.* If New York was the woman's ultimate destination, did he intend to follow her part of or all the way there? In an obsessive frame of mind, he was capable of it. He would go to any ends to bring a felon to justice, collect a debt, and redeem his wounded pride.

Then there was the Featherstone file. *No time to deliver report to client as promised. Regret task is now yours.* Well, that was typical of him. Rush off with hardly any explanation on what might well turn out to be a wild-goose chase, leaving her to deal with his unfinished business.

Will make it up to you upon return. Your Devoted Servant. As though that were enough to excuse his cheekiness and mollify her. Lord, he could be exasperating at times!

Yet, despite all of this, she couldn't help worrying about his welfare. And should he be gone any appreciable length of time, she knew she would miss him. There had been times during their association when his frequent absences and escapades troubled her little or not at all. Now . . . well, now they did. It had been only three days since she'd last seen him, yet already it seemed much longer than that.

"Are you or aren't you in love with John?" Callie had asked her at lunch. She had evaded the question by admitting that she was fond of him but that the only man she had ever loved was Stephen. Which was true and always would be. What she felt for John was not at all the same thing. And yet . . .

Oh, damn! Stop maundering. There's work to be done, this file to be delivered.

She telephoned Sutton Securities Incorporated. Yes, Mr. Sutton was still there; she spoke to him briefly, saying that her partner had been unexpectedly called out of town but that he had completed his report before leaving and she would bring it to him immediately. This satisfied him, though he grumbled again about the delay. She would have to make an effort to placate him further when she arrived.

But she was delayed in leaving the office and making the delivery. For she was just putting on her coat and hat when the door popped open and Fenton Egan came striding in.

Sabina's first thought was that the importer had come to pursue his lecherous interest in her. Egan had other business on his mind, however; one long look at him told her that. His jaw was set in tight lines, the gray eyes sparking instead of caressing. One of his green-and-brown panatelas, unlit, protruded from a corner of his mouth, and there was a dusting of gray ash on his imperial from one previously smoked.

"I've come about my wife," he said in a flat voice.

"What about your wife, Mr. Egan?"

"When did you last see her?"

"You know the answer to that. Tuesday afternoon at your home."

"You didn't see her again later that day?"

"I would have said so if I had. Why are you asking?"

He ignored the question. "The maid told me you came calling again on Wednesday."

"I did, and was told that your wife was unavailable."

"Why the second visit? What did you want with her?"

"You know the answer to that, too."

"I told you in no uncertain terms that neither she nor I was behind the alleged attack on Amity Wellman —"

"Not alleged, actual," Sabina said. "I was there at the time. And no, I don't necessarily suspect her. Or you. I am merely trying to find out who is responsible."

"Well, it wasn't Prudence. And it certainly wasn't me. Your interference in our lives amounts to harassment."

An improper claim, but there was nothing to be gained in arguing the point with him. "Exactly why are you here asking about your wife, Mr. Egan?"

"She's gone missing, that's why."

"Missing? Since when?"

"She left home late Tuesday afternoon, not long after your impudent conversation with her. I haven't seen or heard from her since."

"Nor has anyone else has, I take it."

"Not the maid. Not any of her acquaintances."

"She has no close friend she might have confided in?"

"No."

"Then she certainly wouldn't have confided in me," Sabina said. "I have no idea where she is or why she went away."

"So you say."

"I am not in the habit of lying, sir."

"Well, you must have said or done something on Tuesday that drove her away. There is no other earthly reason for her to have disappeared so suddenly."

"I neither said nor did anything to provoke her."

"So you say," Egan repeated, his mustache bristling.

"Has your wife ever left home unexpectedly before?"

"Never. She's devoted to me."

As if her disappearance were a personal affront. "Have you reported her missing to the police?"

"Certainly not. I have no intention of taking such a drastic step unless absolutely necessary."

"Drastic?"

"It would only cast aspersions on the good name of Egan."

Sabina's dislike of the man, tempered by the news he'd brought, had returned in full. He wasn't so much concerned about his wife's well-being as he was about the possibility of scandal, the innuendo that his wife had abandoned him, and the effect it would have on his image and his business standing. Prudence Egan might be devoted to him, though that was questionable, but the only person Fenton Egan was devoted to was himself.

"You'll get nowhere making unfounded accusations against my methods or my integrity, Mr. Egan," Sabina said crisply. "There is nothing I can tell you or do for you."

He was silent for a few seconds, masticating his cigar. Some of the angry light dimmed in the gray eyes, giving them the look of cold ashes. "All right. Perhaps I was mistaken in my presumption. But goddamn it, woman, I'm at my wit's end."

"I don't appreciate being cursed at. Or being addressed pejoratively as 'woman.' "

"That's what you are, isn't it?"

"Among other things, all of them commanding of respect."

The corner of his mouth containing the panatela lifted in a half-formed sneer.

"I'm sorry your wife has vanished," Sabina said with more restraint than she felt, "but she must have had a good reason for leaving and three days is not a long time. She may have returned home already, for all you know. If she is still missing tomorrow, I suggest you set aside your concerns about 'the good name of Egan' and consult with the authorities. Now I'll thank you to leave, sir. Immediately."

He glowered at her. There wasn't a trace of the seductive charm, the predatory lothario he had exhibited in his office at Bradford and Egan; in a sense he stood naked before her, his true vindictive, phlegmatic, self-involved nature revealed in all its unsavoriness. Then, abruptly, he turned on his heel and stomped out.

Sabina finished fastening her hat with her favorite Charles Horner pin, wondering again how a woman as bright as Amity could be fooled by such a man. She herself had seen through him at their first meeting, although admittedly she had had advance warning. But then, loneliness and physical attraction were powerful temptations that could lead even the most intelligent individual to don temporary blinders.

She waited long enough to allow Egan to leave the building, then left herself to deliver the Featherstone file to Cornelius Sutton.

17

QUINCANNON

The night's unexpected events aboard the *Captain Weber* and a scant few hours of restless sleep combined to put Quincannon in a foul humor come morning. Awake at dawn, he dressed straightaway and left the cabin. The day was dull gray with swarming clouds, the wind blustery and cold again — weather that worked to his advantage, for it allowed him to once more hide most of his bearded face with his high-wrapped muffler and low-pulled cap. Warm beverages and bakery goods were available in the Social Hall, where only a handful of other early risers had gathered, none of them his quarry or her guest. He drank as much coffee as he could hold, then went out on deck and occupied himself in alternately pacing and standing at the starboard rail astern in a pretense of watching their course past long stretches of broad, yellowish farmland and banks thickly grown with willows, tangles of wild grape, and mistletoe-festooned cotton-woods.

They had come out of the last of the snakelike bends in the river and were on the long reach to Stockton when Buffalo Coat appeared with his possibles bag and entered the Social Hall. Quincannon was close enough to get a better look at him by daylight. His guess of the previous night was accurate: no older than thirty-five, a powder keg of a man with short stubby arms and legs and a large head that seemed to sit squarely on his shoulders. Faugh! Either Pauline Dupree had tastes in men that included the coarse and ugly or he was another of her dupes. Perhaps both.

It was only when the *Captain Weber* whistled her final approach that Dupree herself ventured out on deck with her carpetbag. Quincannon spied her as she went to stand at the starboard rail, again wearing the distinctive red-and-gold cape and ostrich-plume hat. She stood looking downriver, paying no attention to him or any of the other passengers now abroad.

Buffalo Coat emerged from the Social Hall shortly afterward, but instead of joining her he stood at the rail amidships. Not to be seen together in the light of day, evidently. Which would seem to indicate that once ashore they would go their separate ways.

The *Captain Weber* docked at the landing at the foot of Stockton's Center Street, the gangplank was lowered, and the deckhouse passengers began to descend and then to disembark. The actress was among the first group, again refusing a deckhand's offer of aid with her carpetbag. Buffalo Coat followed at a distance, Quincannon fairly close behind him.

Horse-drawn streetcars and a line of hansom cabs waited on the street. It was no surprise that Dupree made straight to the cab at the front. Buffalo Coat went to join the queue waiting to board one of the streetcars. Quincannon had the darkly fanciful wish that he could divide himself in two, so that he could follow the man as well as his quarry. He was keen to know what the lad was up to — but even more keen to find out where the actress was bound.

As her cab drove away, he hurried to the next in line. Feigning breathlessness, he said to the driver, "Dratted woman! Couldn't wait for me, blast her."

"How's that, sir?"

"My wife. We had a spat just before landing and off she went in a huff without telling me our exact destination. She handles all the details when we travel, you see. That's her in the cab that just departed. Would you be so good as to follow? There'll be an extra half-dollar in it for you."

The cabbie, probably married himself, had no objections. He gigged his horse and they clattered out onto Center Street.

Quincannon knew that Stockton had grown appreciably during the past decade, but since his last trip here four years ago it seemed to be still sprouting. It was now a major transportation and commercial center, its economy driven by flour mills, carriage and wagon factories, iron foundries, farm machinery, and shipyards. Buildings newly erected and in various stages of construction dotted the route into the city center and throughout the downtown.

Pauline Dupree's destination turned out to be East Main Street and the Yosemite Hotel. A block square, containing two hundred rooms in two stories set above a gallery-windowed main floor, its roof surmounted by a huge American flag, the Yosemite was considered Stockton's finest hostelry. She departed from her cab at the main entrance. Quincannon, pretending clumsiness, fumbled coins from his change purse to give her time to enter the hotel before he paid the hack driver and followed.

Quincannon shook his head at the door porter, rebuffing him as Dupree had, for she still had her carpetbag in hand as she approached the front desk. Casually, as if examining the lobby's reasonably lavish furnishings, he moved to a vantage point behind one of numerous urn-encased palms and philodendrons distributed about the lobby. As far as he could tell from a distance, Dupree either was engaging a room or had already done so by wire; he watched her complete the registration and receive a key. But instead of heading for the bank of elevators, she carried her bag through the open glass doors to the dining room, where breakfast was evidently still being served.

Quincannon bought a copy of the Stockton *Record* from a lobby vendor, then found a velvet plush chair partially concealed by another of the potted plants from where he had an oblique look into the dining room. The actress sat at a dining table near one of the windows, fortunately with her back to the lobby. His mouth began to water as he watched her linger over whatever repast she'd ordered; he made an effort to force his mind away from food.

Resign yourself, John lad, he told himself. *It's likely to be some while before you're able*

213

to partake of another meal yourself.

When Pauline Dupree rose after finishing her breakfast, he raised the newspaper above eye level and peeked around its edges as she reentered the lobby. This time, looking neither left nor right, she went straight to the elevator bank. Once she was inside one of the cars with the door closed, he stood quickly and drifted over there. The indicator arm above the door told him her room was on the top floor.

He resumed his surveillance in a different chair shaded by a different and somewhat larger plant. More than an hour passed, sufficient time for her to have bathed and changed clothes if she intended to go out again. But no, that was not her intention — not yet, at any rate. Another half hour crept away, during which he finished reading the newspaper. Waiting in her room for someone, mayhap Buffalo Coat, or Noah Rideout if he were here in Stockton rather than on Schyler Island. Or for it to be time to keep an appointment elsewhere —

A voice at his elbow said, "Excuse me, sir."

He looked up to see a towheaded uniformed bellboy not long out of his teens. "Yes?"

"Mr. Potter would like to speak to you."

"Mr. Potter?"

"The desk clerk, sir."

Quincannon ambled over to the desk, removing his cap but leaving his muffler wound up over his chin. The clerk, who could barely lay claim to having a chin, gave him a down-the-nose look and then ran his gaze from the muffler down over the buttoned chesterfield.

"Touch of the grippe," Quincannon lied.

"Pity," the clerk lied. "But the lobby of our establishment is hardly a place to nurse an illness."

The comment pricked Quincannon's temper. He managed to restrain a sharp retort. "That is not why I'm here," he said.

"Indeed? Do you wish to engage a room, Mr. . . . ?"

"Flint, James Flint. I'm not sure yet."

"Not sure?"

"Do you know Noah Rideout? Prominent businessman and farmer on Schyler Island in the delta."

"An unusual name. And not familiar to me."

Which told Quincannon that the Yosemite was not Rideout's choice of hotels whenever he had occasion to visit Stockton. What it didn't tell him was whether or not Pauline Dupree was planning a tryst with Rideout or if she had some other reason for engaging the room.

He said, "I am supposed to meet Mr. Rideout here today on business, but it wasn't made clear just when the meeting is to take place. Or if we'll be spending the night or returning to the delta on the night packet. Would you mind if I waited in the lobby for him?"

Tiny frown lines radiated from the corners of the clerk's eyes. "You don't know where to reach the gentleman?" he asked.

"No, I don't."

"What time will he be arriving?"

"Sometime today, that is all I can tell you. Very sketchy plans, I know, but our arrangement was made in quite a hurry."

"You wish to remain in the lobby until he arrives?"

"As long as necessary, yes." Quincannon produced a silver dollar from his purse and, along with it, a pleading look. "You understand my dilemma, I'm sure. It is really quite important that I meet with Mr. Rideout."

The clerk looked disdainfully at the coin. "Really, sir," he said, but the tenor of his voice and a hint of avarice in his pale eyes belied the disdain.

Reluctantly, Quincannon added another silver dollar. And then a third, the necessity for which caused his blood pressure to rise — the amount of money he was wasting on tips and bribes offended his thrifty Scot's nature — before the clerk made the coins disappear and gave his permission.

Quincannon started to turn away, then reversed himself to ask, "Was that Miss Pauline Dupree who checked in earlier? The statuesque young woman in the red-and-gold cape."

"Yes. It was."

"I thought I recognized her, being from San Francisco myself. Perhaps she'll join Mr. Rideout and me for a cocktail this evening. What room is she in?"

"I am not at liberty to give out that information. Hotel policy, which mustn't be breached. Not for any consideration," he added meaningfully. "If you like, I can have a message delivered to her."

"Later, perhaps."

Quincannon resumed his vigil. Noon came and went. So did various and sundry guests and other individuals, none of them Pauline Dupree. The hotel's central heating made him uncomfortable in his heavy clothing; he had no choice but to unbutton his coat, lower the muffler, and remove the cap to avoid marinating in sweat. The chinless clerk kept casting disapproving looks in his direction, as if he was thinking of reneging on their bribery pact. That annoyance, along with boredom, restlessness, and frustration, deepened Quincannon's irascibility. He bought the current issue of the *Police Gazette,* but the magazine did little to make the creeping passage of time more tolerable. One o'clock came and went. One-thirty —

Buffalo Coat entered the lobby.

Quincannon straightened in his chair, watching the man cross to the front desk without so much as a glance in his direction. At some point Buffalo Coat had acquired another piece of luggage, a black leather satchel. He spoke briefly to the chinless clerk, who then, apparently answering a request, provided him with a sheet of hotel stationery, an envelope, and pen and ink. He transferred the satchel to his left hand, as if he was reluctant to set it down, and proceeded to write. The message was relatively brief: he used only one side of the paper. When he was finished he folded the sheet, sealed it inside the envelope, and handed the envelope and a coin to the clerk. After which he quickly left the hotel.

By Godfrey! That black satchel was similar to the one Titus Wrixton had given to Raymond Sonderberg and, unless Quincannon missed his guess, had similar contents —

money extorted, this time from Noah Rideout. The same villainous game worked in the same fashion, with Buffalo Coat assuming the go-between role here as Sonderberg had in San Francisco. But why hadn't he delivered the payoff to Dupree? Why the writing of the note and a swift exit instead?

Quincannon itched to follow Buffalo Coat, perhaps to eventually confront him and retrieve the swag, but such would have been a mistake. His suppositions were just that, suppositions. Even if the satchel contained a large amount of cash, he had no proof that it had been nefariously obtained and hence no justification for either confiscating it or yaffling Buffalo Coat. Besides which, his primary quarry was still and to the finish Pauline Dupree.

He stayed put, watching the clerk summon the towheaded bellboy and hand him the envelope. The bellboy put it on a silver tray and took it into one of the elevator cars. Assuming the message was for the actress, and a probable assumption it was, Quincannon was eager to find out what she would do once she read it.

Except that as far as he was able to discern she did nothing. The bellboy reappeared shortly, but not Dupree. Not in the next half hour, nor in the next after that.

Quincannon's disgruntlement increased twofold. While the clerk was busy with a small group of newly arrived guests, he sought out the bellboy. As with most of the lad's breed, his tongue was easily loosened by yet another coin from Quincannon's purse.

"Yes, sir," he said, after a covert glance at the front desk. "It was Miss Dupree I delivered the envelope to."

"What room does she occupy?"

"Two-seventy-two."

"Were you present while she read the message in the envelope?"

"On my way out. She seemed kind of upset."

"Did she, now."

"She made a funny little noise and I heard her say . . . well, an unladylike word, sir."

So the message had upset her, had it? A falling out among thieves? A double cross of some sort, such as Buffalo Coat laying claim to all or part of the loot?

But still, she remained in her room. An array of women passed through the lobby, among them a pink-outfitted matron leading a mastiff on a gold chain leash and a Catholic nun in full habit, but there was no sign of Pauline Dupree. Four o'clock vanished. The bumptious clerk was replaced by

220

another, apparently without anything having been said about the daylong presence of Mr. James Flint; the new clerk paid no attention to him.

Five o'clock. Five-thirty. A quarter of six.

Quincannon was in a lather by then. Lack of food and the enforced sitting had given him a pounding headache, not to mention a sore backside; his body felt as if he'd taken a steam bath with his clothes on, and his brain seethed with impotent fury.

At ten minutes to six by the Seth Thomas lobby clock, he threw caution to the wind, hoisted himself out of the chair, picked up his valise, and stalked to the elevators. He'd had his fill of this useless game of all cat and no mouse. The time had come to confront Pauline Dupree again, tell her what he knew and suspected about her liaisons with Noah Rideout and Buffalo Coat, and damn the consequences.

On the second floor he found his way to room 272 and rapped on the door, intending to claim bellboy status and the arrival of another message. The ruse went unused, however, for there was no response from within. He rapped again, then a third time. Silence. And the door stayed shut.

The hallway was deserted in both directions. Tight-lipped, he took from his pocket the pouch containing his set of lockpicks. It took no more than a minute to trip the tumblers in the door lock.

The room was empty.

Empty of not only Pauline Dupree but her carpetbag as well.

Quincannon unleashed an inventive string of oaths fiery enough to have melted brimstone — but only in his mind. A quick search of the room and adjoining bath revealed none of the actress' belongings, nor the note she had received from Buffalo Coat; the only signs of her occupancy were the slightly mussed pillows and counterpane on the four-poster bed and the faint lingering scent of lavender perfume.

The contents of the message must have been responsible for her departure. And she must have left the hotel by way of the back stairs. But why? The obvious answer was that she had spotted him somehow, but he was reluctant to accept that explanation. His mastery of the art of trailing a suspect was second to none; at no point last night or today had he done anything to draw her attention. And she had no reason to suspect she was being followed. Unless Wrixton had decided to make one last effort to convince her not to leave San Francisco and had told her of the conversation at the Reception bar . . . No, the banker had been too resigned, too mired in gloom, to attempt an exercise in further futility. All of his lovesick blandishments had been expended the previous night.

Whatever her reason for the surreptitious leave-taking, it surely involved Buffalo Coat and that satchel he'd carried. It followed, then, that where she'd gone was where she expected to find him. Elsewhere in Stockton? Kennett's Crossing?

Quincannon quit the room, leaving the door unlocked, and went downstairs to the front desk. The night clerk was more accommodating and less greedy than the chinless day clerk, making it unnecessary to part with another bribe in order to obtain information.

Quincannon's first question was "Was Miss Dupree's bill paid in advance?"

"Why do you ask, sir?"

"She and I are . . . acquainted. If she hasn't paid herself . . . well, I'm sure you understand."

The clerk was no stranger to the discreet affairs of hotel guests. After consulting her account, he said, "You needn't be concerned. She paid when she checked in."

"For one night's lodging?"

"Yes, sir."

So she hadn't skipped out on her bill. And the fact that she had booked her room for only one night and now abandoned it indicated that she had no intention of remaining in Stockton. Chances were she had booked passage on one of this evening's night packets, all of which would have left by this hour. If she was already on her way to Sacramento, he might never track her down. But if her destination was the San Joaquin Delta and Kennett's Crossing, where Buffalo Coat had kept his rendezvous with her, there might still be a chance of finding her.

Quincannon asked about other means of transportation to the island backwater. One was by stage, a slow and circuitous route that required a change of equipage in Walnut Grove. The other was by private carriage or horseback on the series of levee roads and ferries that connected the delta islands and sloughs. *Bah!* There was only one daily stage to Walnut Grove, the clerk told him, and it departed midafternoon. And with dusk already settling, it would be foolishly risky to attempt to traverse unfamiliar levee roads in the dark of night.

Despite all the irritants, Quincannon's resolve to put an end to Pauline Dupree's criminal career was stronger than ever. Yes, and he was hungry enough after the day's privation to eat a chunk of whang leather. He entered the dining room and proceeded to gorge himself on a five-course meal. Afterward, puffing furiously on his briar, he took an elevator to the second floor and locked himself inside Room 272.

If by some miracle Dupree did return tonight, he would be there to welcome her. And if she didn't, he would salvage what he could from this Stockton debacle by spending the night free of charge in the blasted woman's room.

18

SABINA

What John would have called woman's intuition, what he himself referred to as a hunch, and what Sabina considered a flash of insight sent her downtown on Saturday morning.

Cleghorne's Floral Delights was open, naturally, and doing a healthy business. Ross Cleghorne, outfitted in one of his impeccably tailored if questionably hued suits (this one was the color of plum pudding), noticed her immediately and favored her with one of his charismatic smiles, but it was some minutes before he finished consummating a sale to an elderly matron and made his way to Sabina's side.

"A pleasure to see you again so soon, dear Mrs. Carpenter. A pleasure indeed. And what may I do for you this fine morning?"

It wasn't a fine morning, as a matter of fact. Thick, wind-swirled fog once more laid a damp gray pall over the city. More rain was in the offing, too; Sabina sensed it and had brought her umbrella with her. But she remained hopeful that the storm would hold off until after this evening's benefit in Union Square.

She said in a lowered tone, "Prudence Egan."

"Ah." He took Sabina's arm and ushered her behind a display of one of his larger and fancier floral creations, an arrangement of red and yellow roses enhanced by seashells and small pieces of driftwood tinted different pastel colors. The scent of the roses, combined with that of dozens of other flower arrangements on exhibit, was cloyingly sweet.

"The location of the lady's pied-à-terre, I surmise?" he said then.

The question and his usual sly look reassured her he had not yet learned that Mrs. Egan had gone missing. "Yes. Were you able to find out?"

"I was indeed. Not an easy task, mind you. Not an easy task at all considering the, ah, sensitive nature of the information. You'll tell no one where you obtained it, of course?"

"Of course. And you'll tell no one who asked you for it."

"Of course. As always, we understand each other perfectly." Mr. Cleghorne beamed at her. After which he said, not at all irrelevantly, "I have designed a splendid new spring confection that I'm sure you will find appealing. Yes, absolutely sure of it."

"How much, may I ask?"

"For you, dear lady, half of what I would charge a less favored customer. A paltry sum, really. You won't be disappointed."

Not in the floral confection, perhaps, but it remained to be seen if the usefulness of the information justified the cost. She said, "Very well. The location, Mr. Cleghorne?"

"Ah, of the pied-à-terre. Larkin Street. Not the best neighborhood, but then hardly a shabby one."

"Where on Larkin Street?"

"Number twenty-four forty-two. A small apartment discreetly tucked away behind an establishment called the Lady Bountiful Salon at twenty-four forty."

"You're certain of this?"

He pretended to be mildly offended. "My dear lady, have I ever led you astray on any subject?"

"No," she admitted, "you haven't."

"Nor will I, ever." He smiled his unctuous smile and rubbed his hands together. "I shall prepare the masterful spring confection for you at once, shall I?"

"You still haven't told me the price."

"For you, dear lady, half of what I would charge anyone else. A mere twelve dollars."

Another of Mr. Cleghorne's literal steals. Sabina managed not to wince, nodding instead.

"Excellent! Shall I have it delivered?"

"Yes. To my home address, please."

"You may expect it before the end of the day. And for you, dear Mrs. Carpenter, the delivery charge will be only one dollar."

The Lady Bountiful Salon, one of several small businesses along that section of Larkin Street, appeared to cater to women of modest income and social standing — a perfect cover for a wealthy Pacific Heights wife's trysting place. The salon was not crowded on this late Saturday morning, nor were its neighboring establishments, the weather being as uncertain as it was. Along one side of the building, an unpaved carriageway debouched into an untenanted cul-de-sac at the rear. Only two structures stood in these confines, an open and empty carriage shed and, behind and detached from the salon, a small cottage-like building with an unprepossessing façade. Obviously this was 2442, though neither door nor front wall bore the number.

Three steps led up to the door. Sabina climbed them, her body bent against the damp wind that swirled through the cul-de-sac, and rapped on the panel with her gloved hand. There was no answer. Three more raps produced the same lack of response. On impulse she tested the latch, expecting to find it locked.

It wasn't. There was an audible click and the door moved inward slightly under her hand.

She hesitated, glancing behind her. The cul-de-sac remained deserted. Quickly she pushed the door open, stepped through.

The odor that assailed her was strong enough to make her catch her breath.

Only once before during her professional life had she smelled anything like it, but that was more than enough to ensure that it could never be forgotten. Her stomach recoiled; she closed her throat against the rise of her gorge. From inside her bag she pinched out a lace handkerchief and held it over her nose and mouth as she moved farther inside.

Gloom coated the interior, the only windows tightly curtained. After a few seconds while her eyes adjusted, Sabina made out a table with a lamp atop it. She went there, found matches, and lit the wick — steeling herself for what the light would reveal.

The remains of Prudence Egan lay twisted on her back before a brocade-covered settee, one of only a few pieces of commonplace furniture. Blood stained the breast of what looked to be the same blue tailor-made suit the woman had worn on Tuesday afternoon. At the end of one outflung arm lay a small-caliber pistol, the tip of her index finger bent inside the trigger guard. Sabina ventured close enough to determine that Mrs. Egan had been stabbed, not shot — a single slash that must have penetrated her heart. The bloody tear in the shirtwaist below the wound indicated an underhand, upward thrust. An overturned chair and items that had been dislodged from a table next to the settee testified to a struggle before the fatal blow was struck.

Dead for several days, likely since sometime Tuesday.

Sabina fought down the urge to flee from the noxious odor of decomposition, hurried through an open doorway into what appeared to be the pied-à-terre's only other room, a bedroom. The bed was neatly made, the counterpane smooth and unwrinkled. A wardrobe contained a small amount of clothing — dresses, skirts, shirtwaists, undergarments, and in one drawer a man's black sweater and cap. There was nothing else except for a nightstand and a catchall table, each bearing a small lamp with a fringed shade.

Sabina hesitated in the doorway, surveying the main room. Nothing caught her eye except for the dead woman and the pistol. As much as she wanted to leave, to breathe the cold, moist air outside, she went instead to where the pistol lay. She knelt, drew a deep breath, picked up the weapon. In doing so, she noticed a long, evidently recent gouge along the sides of both gate and barrel. She held the muzzle to her nose long enough to determine that it had not been fired, then replaced the pistol in the exact position in which it had been before, with Prudence Egan's finger touching the trigger guard.

Sabina was about to rise when something nearby that glinted in the lamplight caught her eye. A small, sharp-pointed piece of metal perhaps three-quarters of an inch long — the tip of a knife or dagger blade, she judged, an old one from the look of the metal. Very old. It was age stained, but it bore no trace of blood. She wrapped it in her handkerchief, taking and holding a deep breath as she did so, then quickly stood, switched off the lamp she'd lit, and made her exit.

The cul-de-sac was as deserted as before. Sabina stood breathing in great gulps of cold air until her head cleared and her stomach stopped doing nip-ups. Then she carefully folded the handkerchief to protect the broken knife tip and returned it to her bag.

Now she faced a quandary. On the one hand, if she reported Prudence Egan's death to the police she would not only face a lengthy and likely unpleasant interrogation, but the details of Amity's affair and the attempt on her life would come to light also. Homer Keeps and his unscrupulous brethren would have a field day. Such publicity would do serious damage not only to Amity, her marriage, and her fight for woman suffrage, but to Sabina's professional reputation as well; Keeps would see to that. It might not be possible to keep a scandal under wraps in any case, but it was worth the effort to try.

But on the other hand, she couldn't simply do nothing. The longer the dead woman remained undiscovered, the worse the situation inside would become. Allowing that to happen would be callous, irresponsible, downright heartless, and she was none of those things.

She hit upon a solution on her way back downtown. It was not a completely satisfactory compromise but appropriate enough under the difficult circumstances and a tolerable salve to her conscience. At the agency she found a sheet of notepaper and an envelope that did not bear the Carpenter and Quincannon name. On the paper she wrote in a sloping backhand that was nothing like her normal handwriting:

Your missus has herself a secret hideaway behind beauty salon at 2440 Larkin Street.

A friend

She penned Fenton Egan's name and the words *Very Important* on the envelope in the same disguised hand, sealed the note inside, and put it into her bag. At Slewfoot's newsstand on the corner of Market and Third, she paid the vendor ten dollars to have one of his trusted couriers deliver the envelope to the Egan residence in Pacific Heights. Even if the importer was not at home, the message would soon enough reach and be read by him. Sabina had no doubt that he would take immediate action to verify its authenticity.

The Voting Rights for Women benefit was reasonably successful. Attendance wasn't quite as large as had been hoped for — though the rain held off, the churning fog was as wet as drizzle — but those who braved the weather were enthusiastic and generous. Most were women, naturally, running the gamut from shabbily dressed clerks and laundresses and scullery maids to fur-clad matrons from the upper-class neighborhoods, but there were more than a few male supporters as well. Amity's impassioned speech brought cheers and resounding applause. Donations to the cause, from nickels and dimes to more than one five-dollar gold piece, amounted to upward of one hundred dollars.

Nathaniel Dobbs and his sign-carrying Antis were also there, of course, but their number was surprisingly few. And every time Dobbs attempted to interrupt the proceedings with one of his opposition rants he was shouted down and roundly booed.

Sabina's decision to say nothing yet to Amity or Elizabeth about the violent death of Prudence Egan had been the right one.

19

QUINCANNON

It was midafternoon on Sunday when the Southern Pacific steamboat *Delta Queen* whistled for her arrival at Kennett's Crossing. Quincannon, standing at the deckhouse rail with his valise in hand, had a clear view of the sorry little backwater as the packet drew up to the landing.

The hamlet's buildings were all on the southwest side of a wide body of brownish water colorfully and no doubt accurately named Dead Man's Slough. On both sides of the slough, a few hundred yards from where it merged with the broad expanse of the San Joaquin River, a raised levee road ended at a cable-operated ferry landing; the barge was presently anchored on this bank, next to a ramshackle ferryman's shack built close to the edge of a thin rind of mud and cattails. A pair of large bells on wooden standards, one at each landing, were what travelers used to summon the tender when the ferry barge was on the opposite bank.

On this side the inn, a long, weathered structure built partly on solid ground and partly on thick pilings, stood next to the levee road. The rest of Kennett's Crossing ran upward in a ragged line to where the slough narrowed and vanished among tangles of swamp growth and stunted oaks choked with wild grapevine. Its sum was approximately a dozen buildings and several shantyboats and houseboats tied to the bank alongside a single sagging wharf.

Quincannon was the only passenger to disembark. As soon as he stepped off, deckhands raised the gangplank and the *Delta Queen*'s whistle sounded again and her stern buckets immediately began to churn the river water to a froth. There was no sign of anyone abroad as he strode up the road to the inn. Scuds of dark-bellied clouds gave the place an even bleaker aspect, like a bad landscape painting done in chiaroscuro. The smell of ozone was sharp in the air. There would be rain by nightfall.

Two men were in the inn's common room, a giant with a black beard twice as bushy as Quincannon's and an old man with a glass eye and fierce expression, who slouched with hands on hips before a minimally stocked liquor buffet. They appeared to have been engaged in an argument, which ended abruptly upon Quincannon's entrance. His deduction that the giant was the innkeeper proved to be correct; the gent's name was Adam Kennett.

"Is it food, lodging, or both you'll be wanting, mister?"

"Neither at the moment. It's information I'm after."

"What information would that be?"

It was overly warm in the room; heat pulsed from a glowing potbellied stove. Quincannon opened his chesterfield and unwound his muffler before speaking. "Did a woman arrive on one of the night boats from Stockton last night?" he asked. "Young, handsome, blond haired."

"Young? Handsome? Phooey!" This came grumblingly from the old man. "Ain't nobody like that in this miserable excuse for a town. Never has been, never will be."

"I'll have no more of that, Mr. Dana," Kennett said.

Dana glared at him with his good eye. "An outrage, that's what I call it. A damned outrage."

"Watch your language. I won't tell you again."

"I'm a veteran, by grab, I served with McClellan's Army of the Potomac in the War Between the States. I'm entitled to a drink of whiskey when I have the money to pay for it."

"The buffet is temporarily closed," Kennett explained to Quincannon. "And for good reason."

"Good reason my hind end. Not a drop of spirits sold on account of religion, and me with a parched throat. It ain't right, I tell you. I ain't Catholic. I ain't even a believer."

"Well, I am."

Quincannon said, "If the woman I described did arrive by steamer last night, would you be aware of it, Mr. Kennett?"

"No. I don't stand down at the landing in the middle of the night, or the middle of the day, neither. Folks come to me if they want food or lodging. I don't go looking for them."

"Do you know a local man given to wearing a long buffalo coat?"

"That's like asking if I know a local man wears galluses. Buffalo coats ain't what you'd call uncommon around here."

"Short, squat, large head, hardly any neck. Thirty-five or so."

"That sounds like Gus Burgade," the old man said.

Kennett shrugged. "Could be."

"Who is Gus Burgade?" Quincannon asked.

"Runs a store boat, the *Island Star.* Puts up here sometimes when he's not out making his rounds."

Store boats, small in number, prowled the fifteen hundred square miles of sloughs and islands between Sacramento and Stockton, peddling everything from candy to kerosene to shantyboaters, small farmers, field hands, and other delta denizens. More than one of their owners were reputed to be less than honest. "Was the *Island Star* here night before last?"

"Sure it was," Dana said. "Gone yestiday morning, though."

"Due back when, do you know?"

"Later today or tomorrow, likely," Kennett said. "You got business with Burgade?"

"I may have. With Mr. Noah Rideout, too. I take it you're acquainted with him."

"The high-and-mighty farmer?" The innkeeper's voice took on a truculent edge. "I know him to speak to, not that he'll have much truck with the likes of me."

"Goddamn teetotaler," Dana said. "Phooey!"

"I told you before to watch your language, mister. And keep your voice down, too, or

240

out you go."

"Throw me out with foul weather comin', would you? And without so much as one little drink of whiskey to warm my bones."

"One little drink is never enough for you."

"How much whiskey I swallow ain't nobody's business but mine."

Kennett sighed. "Burgade'll have a jug of forty-rod for sale, if you're willing to pay his price."

"I'll pay it, right enough, if he comes today. But I suppose I can't bring the jug back here to sip on where it's warm?"

"No, you can't. Kennett's Inn is a temporary temperance house."

"Temporary temperance house. Phooey." Dana moved away from the buffet, then stopped abruptly to give Quincannon a closer one-eyed scrutiny. "You a Johnny Reb?"

"Johnny Reb? Hardly."

"Southerner, ain't you? Tell by your accent."

The old man must have ears like an elephant to detect what was now only a faint trace of a southern accent. "Born in Baltimore," Quincannon admitted, "but I've lived in San Francisco for fifteen years."

"Once a Johnny Reb, always a Johnny Reb. Spot one of you graybacks a mile away.

Only good Reb's a dead one, you ask me."

"The Civil War has been over for thirty years, Mr. Dana."

"Tell that to my right eye. It's been pining for the left one for more'n thirty years. Damned Reb shot it out at Antietam."

He clumped over to a long puncheon table and sat down with his arms folded and mouth downturned into a lemony pucker.

"Don't mind the old coot," Kennett said to Quincannon. "He's only like that when he's sober and getting ready for a trip to the doctor in San Francisco. His bark's worse than his bite."

"About Noah Rideout, Mr. Kennett. Have you ever seen him in the company of a woman such as the one I described?"

"Can't say I have because I haven't. He minds his business; I mind mine."

"How far is his Schyler Island farm from here?"

"Six, seven miles."

"How do I get to it?"

"You figure on going out there today?"

It was one of two options, the other, less desirable one being to wait here on the chance that Gus Burgade and his store boat would put in an appearance. Action was always preferable to passive waiting. If Pauline Dupree wasn't to be found at the Schyler Island farm, Rideout himself might have returned there by this time.

Quincannon said, "Yes, if I can rent a horse."

"Prob'ly can. Livery's right across the road, Mr. — What'd you say your name was?"

"I didn't. But it's Flint, James Flint."

"Take the ferry across Dead Man's Slough, Mr. Flint, and follow the levee road till you come to another ferry at Irishman's Slough. That one'll take you to Schyler Island." Kennett paused and then advised, "I'd get a move on if I was you — we're in for a blow tonight."

The livery was a barnlike building diagonally up-road from the inn. One of the doors was open and a buttery lamp glow shone within. Entering, Quincannon discovered four horses in stalls and the hostler asleep in the harness room. He woke the man up and questioned him. No, he hadn't rented either a wagon or a horse to a woman answering Pauline Dupree's description — "Never seen anyone looked like that around here, more's the pity" — or to anyone else in the past few days. He'd seen Noah Rideout a few days ago when one of his employees had delivered him to the steamboat landing in a carriage, hadn't seen him since.

Quincannon haggled with the hostler from a distance of two feet — he had a mouth half-full of as many black teeth as white and a rancid breath that would have gagged a goat — and emerged astride the best of the available horses, a ewe-necked bay, his valise tied to the saddle horn.

The last traveler or travelers to use the ferry had been headed west; the barge was moored on the opposite bank of the slough. Quincannon yanked the bell rope on the landing stage and the bell's sharp notes brought the ferryman, a muscular gent of some fifty years, from his shack. He seemed none too happy to be summoned out once again into the chill afternoon; he answered Quincannon's questions about the identity of recent travelers with nothing more than a series of grunts and monosyllables as he winched the scow across. It was held by grease-blackened cables made fast to pilings on a spit of north-side land a hundred yards upslough. The current would push the ferry across from shore to shore, guided by a centerboard attached to its bottom and by the ferryman's windlass.

When the barge nudged the plank landing, the ferryman quickly put hitches in the mooring ropes, then lowered the approach apron so Quincannon could lead the horse aboard. As soon as the ferryman collected the toll, he set the cable to whining thinly on the windlass drum and the scow began moving again, back across. A taciturn cuss, he said not a word the entire time.

The levee road was well graded and fairly well maintained, in order to accommodate wagons, carriages, and stagecoaches, and the bay handled easily; Quincannon set a brisk pace. The wind had sharpened and the clouds were low hanging, so low that the tops of some of the taller trees in the flanking swampland were obscured by their drift. But the ozone smell was no stronger than it had been and there was no moisture in the air yet. The storm was still two or three hours off.

The road was flanked on both sides by streams of sluggish brown water, swamp oaks, and moss-infested sycamores all the way to the next ferry crossing at Irishman's Slough. He met no one along the way. The ferry tender there was less taciturn than the one in Kennett's Crossing; he informed Quincannon as he winched him and the bay across that the only others to request passage today were local farmers. The land on Schyler Island had been cleared and planted with crops; fields of onions and a variety of green vegetables stretched as far as the eye could see. Most of the farmhands tending them were Chinese, so many of which race worked as delta laborers that an entire community had been established at Locke.

A mile or so from the ferry landing, farm buildings appeared in the distance. The entrance to the road that led to them was spanned by a huge, arched wooden sign into which the name **RIDEOUT** had been carved and then gilded. Quincannon turned in there, rode another quarter of a mile through fenced fields to the farmstead.

There were several buildings, all whitewashed and well-kept. The main house was surprisingly large and elaborate for the delta country, two stories of wood and stone with a galleried porch in front. As soon as he reined up in a broad wagonyard, the front door opened and a burly fellow wearing a butternut coat over gray twill trousers came out and down the steps.

He looked Quincannon over appraisingly before asking, "Something I can help you with, mister?"

"I'd like to speak with Mr. Rideout, if he's here."

"He isn't. He's in Stockton on business."

"When is he expected back?"

"Late tonight. If you have business with him, you can tell me what it is. Foster's my name, Mr. Rideout's aide-de-camp."

"Business with him, yes, but of a private sort. Concerning a lady friend of his."

"And who would that be?"

"Pauline Dupree. An actress at the Gaiety Theater in San Francisco."

If Foster recognized the name, his face didn't show it and he didn't admit it. He said nothing.

"Handsome woman, dark gold hair. Mr. Rideout kept company with her in the city."

"His business, if so."

"She wouldn't happen to be here, would she?"

"The only women here are servants." Foster's gaze narrowed. "Who are you? What's your interest in Mr. Rideout and this Dupree woman?"

"I'd rather discuss that with him."

"I'll still have your name, unless you have some reason to withhold it."

"John Quincannon. Which packet will he be on tonight?"

Instead of answering the question, Foster said, "It'll be late when he arrives and he won't want to be disturbed. You'll have to wait until tomorrow to see him."

Not if I have my druthers, Quincannon thought. "Will you be meeting him?"

Foster didn't answer that question, either.

"Tomorrow, Mr. Quincannon. Good day until then."

He turned on his heel and reentered the house.

20

SABINA

Kamiko opened the door to Sabina's ring, Elizabeth hovering close behind her. "Good morning, Mrs. Carpenter," the girl said, bowing but unsmiling.

"Good morning."

"You wish to speak with Amity-san?"

"Yes."

Sabina closed her umbrella, shook the drops of rain from it before entering. Elizabeth said as she stepped inside, "Mrs. Wellman is upstairs changing. We've just come back from church." She added, "Everything here is status quo."

No, it isn't, Sabina thought. "I'll wait for her in the main parlor," she said.

Kamiko took the umbrella from her, placed it inside a copper stand, then hurried across the entryway and up the winding staircase to the second floor.

"Will you want me to join you?" Elizabeth asked.

"No. I need to speak to Amity alone."

"I'll go up and pack my things, then. This *is* my last day here, with Mr. Wellman due home this evening?"

"Yes."

Elizabeth paused. "You seem a bit . . . tense this morning, Sabina. Is something wrong?"

"I'll explain later."

She went across through the archway into the main parlor. The room was cold, logs having been laid on the hearth but not yet set ablaze. The heavy damask curtains were drawn over the windows to mask the dreary gray drizzle outside. One lamp glowed palely; Sabina lifted the glass and put fire to the wick of a second lamp near the display of antique weaponry.

Its glow gave her a clear look into the glass-topped case containing Burton's collection of antique daggers and knives. The ivory-handled *kaiken* in its matching scabbard was in its customary place in the second case. She was just about to lift the lid when Amity entered from the hallway.

"Good morning, Sabina. Not a day for bicycling, is it?"

"No, it isn't." Nor would it be if the sun

were shining.

"Brrr, it's cold in here. I'll light the fire."

While Amity was doing that, Sabina reached into the case and removed the *kaiken.* When she slid it out of its scabbard she saw what she expected to see and had hoped she wouldn't.

The tip of the ancient razor-sharp, double-edged blade was missing.

There was a whooshing sound as the hearth logs burst into flame. Amity turned, saw Sabina holding the *kaiken,* and said, "That handle is beautifully carved, isn't it." But then she came closer and her brows knitted. "What could have happened to the blade? Burton will be furious when he sees that it's been broken off. It's one of his favorite pieces."

"I know what happened to it."

"You do?"

Sabina took the lace handkerchief from her coat pocket, unfolded it, and removed the broken metal tip. It had the same dull patina, the same sharp double edge, as the blade of the *kaiken.* There was no need to fit the tip to the blade; the two were identical.

Bewildered, Amity asked, "Where did you find the broken tip? Here somewhere?"

"No. Before I tell you, I have some questions to ask."

"Questions?"

"About the love letter you received from Fenton Egan. Did it come through the mail or was it hand delivered the same as the threatening notes?"

". . . Through the mail."

"Plain stationery, with no return address on the envelope."

"No, of course not." Frown ridges marred the surface of Amity's forehead. "Sabina, what . . . ?"

"Where did you read the letter? In the entryway?"

"No, in here."

"And you were alone at the time."

"Naturally. I wouldn't have opened the envelope in front of Kamiko."

"Did Egan sign his name to the letter?"

"Yes." Her mouth twist was bitter. " 'With abiding love, Fenton.' "

"And once you read it, you threw it into the fireplace."

"Along with the envelope, just as I told you."

"Was the fire blazing as it is now?"

"Blazing? I don't . . . Why are you asking all these questions, for heaven's sake?"

"Please, Amity. *Was* the fire hot, blazing that day?"

". . . No. It had begun to bank."

"Did you wait to watch the letter and envelope burn?"

"Did I? No. No, I was too upset, with myself as much as with Fenton for writing such a letter. I went upstairs to lie down."

"Where was Kamiko at the time?"

"On her way in here, I suppose to attend to the fire. I passed her in the hallway — Oh, my God! You don't think Kamiko rescued the letter before it burned?"

"That's just what I think. Rescued it and read it."

Her face pale, Amity sank onto one of the damask-covered *estrado* chairs.

"If you're right, then she did know about the affair. That was what she was holding back, hiding. . . ."

"More than just knowledge of the affair."

"What do you mean?"

Sabina hated what she had to do and say next, but there was no way to prolong the necessity or to sugarcoat it. She went to sit next to her friend. "Let's suppose," she said, "that Kamiko did read the letter and was upset by it. She could have confronted you, demanded or begged you to end the affair, but she didn't."

"She's not the sort to demand or beg."

"But neither is she the sort to have tacitly

allowed it to continue. She couldn't bring herself to confront you, it would have been too painful for her, but she felt she had to do something. Not appeal to your lover to end the affair — her Japanese heritage, with its emphasis on female deference to the male, wouldn't have permitted it. But she could appeal to his wife, woman to woman."

"Oh, dear Lord! You mean that's how Prudence Egan found out about the affair? Kamiko betrayed me?"

"She wouldn't have viewed it that way, but as a moral duty in order to preserve your marriage. Only she had no way of knowing then how disturbed and dangerous the Egan woman was, the extent of her rage and hatred. She found out last Sunday evening."

"Then . . . it was Prudence Egan who tried to kill me?"

"Yes. Brooded and brooded and finally crossed the line."

Amity shook her head twice, three times, as if trying to clear jumbled thoughts. "But why didn't Kamiko tell us then what she'd done? She must have realized Prudence Egan could have been the assailant, the danger in continuing to keep silent."

"I think she did. I think she may even have recognized the woman before she fled through the garden. Her night vision is much better than yours and mine."

"And still she kept quiet? She must hate me almost as much as Prudence Egan did —"

"On the contrary, she loves you very much. More than enough to protect you at all costs. That's why she did what she did later."

"What do you mean? What did she do later?"

Sabina drew a breath, let it out slowly. "She should be the one to tell you. Ring for her, Amity."

"But what if she still won't admit —"

"She will. Now."

Amity went to pull the bell rope. Kamiko appeared almost immediately, her small face unsmiling, the luminous black eyes showing an emotion that might have been sadness. Nothing changed in her expression when she saw the *kaiken* Sabina still held in her hand.

"You wish something, Amity-san?"

"Sabina and I want to talk to you. Sit down."

The Japanese girl perched on the settee, knees together under her kimono, slippered feet flat on the floor, small hands clasped together in her lap. Her gaze shifted slowly between the two women. She must have known what was coming; the tension in the room was palpable, and the few moments of silence had a brittle quality. Yet her delicate features remained impassive.

"It's time for the truth, Kamiko, the whole truth," Sabina said. "No more secrets."

"And please, no lies," Amity added.

"You know I do not lie."

"Did you save a letter to me from burning in the fireplace last week? And then read it?"

"Yes." Without hesitation. "I should not have, I know."

"No, you shouldn't. Nor should you have gone to Mrs. Egan and showed it to her. You did do that, didn't you?"

"To speak with her, yes. But I did not show her the letter. I burned it as you wished."

"Still, you betrayed me." Then, painfully, "As I betrayed Burton, to my everlasting shame."

"My shame is greater than yours, Amity-san," the girl said softly. "Much greater."

"Because you knew it was she who tried to shoot me."

"Yes."

"For another reason, too," Sabina said. "The death of Prudence Egan."

Startled, Amity sucked in her breath. "Prudence Egan is *dead*? How? When, where?"

"Stabbed on Tuesday afternoon in an apartment she rented on Larkin Street." Briefly Sabina explained about the woman's trysting place. "I learned the address and discovered her body there yesterday."

"Yesterday? Why on earth did you wait so long to tell me?"

"I saw no purpose in disrupting the benefit last night. And I needed more time to be sure of my suspicions."

"Stabbed, you said. Dear God! With that *kaiken* knife?"

"Yes."

"Then . . . Kamiko? Oh, no, no —"

Emotion showed in the girl's face for the first time. She clasped her hands together more tightly in her lap. "Yes, it is true," she admitted. "But I did not mean for it to happen."

Sabina said, "The *kaiken* is the traditional weapon favored by Japanese women. You took it with you when you went again to see Mrs. Egan."

"*Hai.* For protection and self-defense. That is the only reason. She was a dangerous woman and I did not know what she might do."

257

"Then why did you risk accusing her?"

"I felt that I must. I believed wrongly, foolishly, that my promise to remain silent would prevent her from another attempt on Amity-san's life."

"You recognized her in the garden Sunday night?"

"I was not positive it was she, but I thought it must be."

Amity said, "But why not tell me or Sabina? Or the police?"

"I could not. I had no proof of her guilt."

So young, so naïve to believe she could reason with the likes of Prudence Egan. Driven by guilt for putting her beloved guardian's life in jeopardy in the first place. Seeking a measure of atonement.

"Tell us what happened Tuesday afternoon, Kamiko."

In a barely audible voice, she told them. She had first gone to see Prudence Egan on Monday, twice that day, but the woman hadn't been home either time. When Kamiko returned again on Tuesday, driving the Wellmans' buggy after finishing her marketing, she arrived just as Mrs. Egan was leaving in a hansom. Kamiko followed the cab to Larkin Street.

Prudence Egan was furious to find the girl on the doorstep of her private hideaway.

When Kamiko made her accusation, the woman grew even more enraged. She took her pistol from a table drawer and advanced on Kamiko, "the flame of madness lighting her eyes." She came so close, her finger whitening on the trigger, that the girl, fearing for her life, drew the *kaiken* from her coat pocket and thrust out with it, not at Mrs. Egan but at the pistol in her hand. The knife struck the weapon with enough force to drive it from her grasp, leaving the long scratch on its surface and at the same time snapping off the tip. To Kamiko's horror, the blade then deflected upward and into the woman's breast. Death must have been instantaneous. As soon as the girl realized Prudence Egan was dead, she fled. Until now she had not been able to speak or even allow herself to think that she had taken a life, even that of a violent madwoman. She was sorry she had done so, so very sorry.

"It was self-defense," Amity said emphatically. She went to sit beside her ward, gently placed an arm around her shoulders. "Sabina?" she said then. "I believe it happened just as Kamiko told it. You do, too, don't you? You believe her?"

Sabina looked at the small figure huddled abjectly in Amity's embrace, her almond-shaped eyes now wet with tears. "Yes," she said, "I believe her."

21

QUINCANNON

It was a long, cold ride from the Rideout ranch back to Kennett's Crossing. But a dry one, at least, the rain continuing to hold off and saving him the misery of traveling muddy levee roads without a slicker to keep from being drenched. Not that the return trip was without discomfort. It had been some time since Quincannon had sat a horse and he was feeling a touch rump sprung by the time he neared Dead Man's Slough.

Sounds carried far in the delta, particularly on days such as this one; even before he reached the ferry landing he could hear, strangely enough, loud music rolling out over the swampland from Kennett's Crossing — a rusty-piped calliope playing an off-key rendition of "The Girl I Left Behind Me."

The calliope stopped its atonal caterwauling just before Quincannon reached the ferry landing. He took advantage of the respite to ring for the closemouthed ferryman and then board the scow, which was still moored on this bank. While he and the bay were being winched across, the calliope started up again. He could tell from midslough where the music, such as it was, was coming from — an old, weather-beaten steamer moored at the town wharf. Doubtless Gus Burgade's store boat, the *Island Star.*

The wind was an icy breath on the open water. Overhead, darkening clouds moved furtively; the smell of rain had grown heavy in the late-afternoon air. The coming storm would break long before whichever Stockton packet Noah Rideout had booked passage on arrived at Kennett's Crossing. There were possible benefits in a stormy night, Quincannon thought, but none where his first meeting with the wealthy rancher was concerned.

When he clattered off the barge's landing apron, he had a better look at the store boat. The calliope was anchored to her foredeck, still giving forth, monotonously, "The Girl I Left Behind Me" — evidently intended as a clarion call to potential customers. If its piping had drawn many, there was no evidence of them now; the *Island Star* likely had been here for some time.

He rode to the livery, turned the bay over to the hostler, then allowed the wind to push him past the inn and along a grassy branch of the levee road toward the wharf. As he drew abreast of the gangplank at the battered little steamer's waist, the old Civil War veteran, Dana, came hurrying out of the lamplit cargo hold, clutching a bottle of forty-rod whiskey. Dana glared at him in passing, muttered something, and scooted off to find a place to do his solitary drinking. He was evidently the last of the store boat's initial wave of customers. No one was visible in the hold and the decks were deserted except for a kanaka deckhand lounging near the rusty calliope.

Quincannon sauntered across the plank, entered the hold. It had been outfitted as a store, with cabinets fastened around the bulkheads, a long counter at one end, and every inch of deck space crammed with a welter of sacks, bins, barrels, boxes, tools, and other loose goods. A barrel of a man outfitted in what looked to be a new linsey-woolsey shirt was perched on a stool behind the counter, a short-six cigar clamped between yellowed teeth.

"Afternoon," he said around the stump of

his stogie. His steady gaze was appraising. There seemed to be no recognition in it, but it was difficult to tell in the dim lantern light. "Help you with something, friend?"

"Would you be Gus Burgade?"

"I would. Owner, captain, and pilot of the *Island Star.*"

And the man who had spent the night in Pauline Dupree's stateroom on the *Captain Weber* and sent her the message at the Yosemite Hotel yesterday afternoon. There was no mistaking the short, stubby arms, small head, powerful torso, and rough-hewn features.

"Flint," Quincannon said, "James Flint."

"Well, Mr. Flint. What can I do for you?"

"A tin of Navy Cut, if you have it."

"Don't. Never had a call for it."

"Cable Twist?"

"Nor that, neither."

"What kind of pipe tobacco do you stock?"

"Virginia plug and Durham loose."

"The plug, then."

Burgade produced a sack of cheap tobacco and named a price that was half again what it would cost anywhere else. Quincannon paid without protest or comment.

"Seems I've seen you somewhere before," Burgade said.

"This is my first visit to Kennett's Crossing."

"Elsewhere, then. Walnut Grove, maybe. Or Stockton."

Quincannon said cautiously, "Mayhap. Though I haven't been to either town in several years."

"Big gent like you, nice dressed, kind of hard to forget. Well, no matter. What brings you here?"

"Business. With a Schyler Island farmer, Noah Rideout."

No reaction to the name. "What kind of business, you don't mind my asking?"

"It concerns a lady friend he met in San Francisco."

Nothing changed in Burgade's expression. "Lady friend, eh? Who would she be?"

"I'm not at liberty to say. Do you know Mr. Rideout?"

"Heard of him, never met him."

"I was supposed to meet him at his farm today," Quincannon said, "but he has been away on business in Stockton and isn't expected back until late tonight."

"So you'll be staying over at Kennett's Inn, will you?"

"No. Mr. Rideout will be met here when he arrives by packet and I expect to return to his farm with him."

No reaction to this, either. Give the rogue credit for unflappability, if nothing else. "Storm due any time now. Bad night for a buggy ride all the way to Schyler Island."

"Worse day tomorrow if the rains continue. The levee road will be a quagmire. You'll be weathering the storm here yourself, I take it?"

"Be a fool not to."

Quincannon had taken the cat-and-mouse conversation to its limit. In fact, he may have taken it too far. It depended on whether Burgade and Pauline Dupree had made contact and, if so, they had settled their differences and divvied up the Rideout extortion money and where she was now and what her plans were. For all Quincannon knew, she was tucked up in a cabin right here on the *Island Star.* Or, worse, a prospect that grated on him like sandpaper, she'd concluded her business with Burgade last night and was on her way to Sacramento, perhaps already there and on board an eastbound train.

"Was there anything else, friend?" Burgade asked him.

He said, "No, friend, nothing," and took his leave.

Restlessly he prowled the meager settlement, but there was nothing there to enlighten him. Shadows had formed and lengthened among the collection of shacks and the surrounding swampland, and with the coming night the heavy concentration of storm clouds began to break open. The first drops of wind-flung rain, cold as ice crystals against his skin, drove him back to the inn.

Rich aromas greeted him as he entered, reminding him that he hadn't eaten since a doughnut on board the *Delta Queen* that morning. The common room was deserted except for Adam Kennett, who was closing the potbellied stove after having added more firewood. Quincannon welcomed the heat this time. He said, "I'd like a room, Mr. Kennett. Whether for a few hours or for the night has yet to be determined," and went to stand warming his backside in front of the stove.

"Price is the same either way. Six bits."

"Including dinner?"

"Quarter extra for meals."

High prices in this tawdry backwater, Quincannon thought grumpily as he paid. Already this chase after Pauline Dupree was costing him dearly, what with steamer passage, hansoms, bribes, tips, meals, and now a night's lodging. Such a continuous outlay without a client to reimburse him would have the lingering effect of an embedded splinter if he failed to locate Pauline Dupree and the money she'd extorted from Titus Wrixton and, likely, from Noah Rideout.

"Supper any time you want it," Kennett said. "Liquor buffet's still closed, sorry to say."

"No matter. I'm not a drinking man."

The bushy-whiskered innkeeper sighed. "I wish I wasn't. Night like this, whiskey's a man's best friend. This man's, anyhow."

Sufficiently warmed, Quincannon found his way down a central corridor at the rear. The room he'd been given was not much larger than a cell, windowless, furnished with a narrow bed and a rust-stained washstand. He deposited his valise on the sagging mattress, drew his Navy Colt to check the loads for the fourth or fifth time the past two days, then went back out to the common room and into what passed for a dining hall.

Guests had no choice when it came to the fare at Kennett's Inn. Supper, served by a Chinese waitress, was a plate of fried catfish, potatoes, and corn and a cup of bitter coffee. Barely palatable, though that didn't stop him from wolfing it all down and requesting a second helping of catfish (another dime, confound it) and a thin slab of peach pie. His appetite had always been prodigious. He had inherited all of his father's lusty appetites, in fact, along with his genteel Virginia-born mother's love of poetry.

Sabina had once remarked that he was a curious mixture of the gentle and the stone hard, the sensitive and the unyielding. He supposed that was an accurate assessment. And the reason, perhaps, that he was a better detective than Thomas L. Quincannon, the rival of Pinkerton in the nation's capital during the Civil War. He knew his limitations, his weaknesses. His father had never once admitted to being wrong on any subject whatsoever but considered himself invincible — and had been prematurely and ignominiously dispatched while on a fool's errand on the Baltimore docks. John Frederick Quincannon intended to die in bed at the age of ninety. And not alone, either.

No one else entered the dining room during his meal. If there were any other guests at the inn, they were forted up in their rooms. The rain was squall heavy now, hammering on the roof, rattling shutters. A night for neither man nor beast. Would the foul weather change Noah Rideout's mind about venturing home tonight? Possibly, though he had already made arrangements with his aide-de-camp to meet him here and had no last-minute way of canceling them.

In his room, Quincannon lit his pipe and tried to read from the volume of *May Day and Other Poems* and then from a second volume of poetry he'd brought with him, Walt Whitman's *Leaves of Grass.* But he was too keyed up to relax tonight. And the verses by Emerson and Whitman made him yearn for Sabina. Only two days away from her and already he missed her company. . . .

He'd never felt this way about a woman before, never believed he was capable of that nebulous emotion called love. A confirmed bachelor, that was John Quincannon, taking his pleasure with as many comely wenches as were willing to provide it — neither a rake nor a monk, but a red-blooded Scot who had always considered marriage a state of entrapment to be avoided at all costs. A lusty loner was how he'd thought of himself before he met Sabina and for some while afterward.

In the beginning his personal interest in her, he now admitted with a sense of shame, had been simple seduction. Her refusal to succumb had been both a challenge and a source of mounting frustration. He couldn't quite pinpoint when having her as a bed partner ceased to be a primary objective and his feelings for her began to evolve to their present state. The process had been gradual, brought about by a deepening respect for her as a woman as well as a detective partner and a desire to spend more and more time in her company outside the confines of the agency. Now he couldn't imagine life without her, personally or professionally.

It was a marvel that she had begun to feel the same. And she must have, else she wouldn't have finally relented and permitted him to squire her about on an increasingly frequent basis. Squiring was all she'd permitted thus far, but that was fine with him. For the nonce, anyway. The greater intimacy he craved was only partly sexual now. His longing went deeper than that, perhaps as deep as a proposal of marriage. But her late husband had been the love of her life, and she had been faithful to his memory in the years since his death. What if she had no interest in marrying again and were to say no to the proposal? What would he do then?

A knock on his door put a merciful end to these thoughts. He opened it to find Adam Kennett. "Sorry to bother you, Mr. Flint," the innkeeper said, "but the storm and the temporary temperance have got me twitchy as the devil. You happen to play chess?"

"Chess? I do, yes. . . ."

"Care for a game or two? Help pass the time on a long night?"

That it would, Quincannon agreed. The fact that the bearded giant played a cerebral game was no less surprising than his proficiency at various gambits. Quincannon played excellent chess himself under normal circumstances, but his attention kept slipping away to Pauline Dupree, Gus Burgade, and Noah Rideout. Kennett won three matches and they stalemated the fourth. Outside, rain continued its furious pounding on the inn's tin roof and the wind moaned and chattered ceaselessly.

It was a few minutes past eleven by Quincannon's watch when they finished the last game. Time to venture out and await the arrival of the Stockton packet. After returning to his room for his valise, he said as much to Kennett, explaining briefly that Noah Rideout was supposed to be arriving on one of the night boats and that he had business with the farmer.

"Supposed to be?" Kennett said as Quincannon donned his chesterfield, muffler, and cap. "You're not sure?"

"Not positively, no."

"Your business with him must be urgent."

"That it is. Very urgent."

The innkeeper made no further comment, though his expression indicated that he thought any man who went out into a fierce late-night blow like this one on an uncertain errand, no matter what his purpose, was something of an addlepate.

22

QUINCANNON

In the wet darkness Quincannon drew the muffler up over his face like a bandit's mask, wishing that he had a slicker rather than the soon-to-be-sodden chesterfield. At least his valise was waterproof. Visibility was no more than a few yards; he could barely make out the daubs of light that marked the ferryman's shack, the brighter glows of the protected hurricane lanterns on the steamboat landing. Wind gusts constantly changed the slant of the rain so that it was like a jiggling curtain against the night's black wall.

Shoulders hunched and body bowed, he set off along the muddy levee road. Its surface was still solid along the edges, but if the rain continued to whack down with this much intensity by morning the road would be a quagmire.

Faint scattered lights materialized here and there in the town buildings, but none shone at the upslough wharf when he detoured in that direction. At first he thought Burgade had lied and the *Island Star* had slipped out of Dead Man's Slough under cover of the storm. But no, she was still moored there, the bumpers roped to her strakes thumping against the pilings as the rough waters rolled her from side to side. All dark as she was, she looked like an abandoned derelict.

Quincannon heeled around, returned to the levee road, and plowed down it past the unlighted ferryman's shack. The steamer landing, he saw as he approached, was deserted. When he entered the landing's rickety lean-to shelter, he startled a bird of some sort, a snipe or plover, and sent it whickering off through the swamp growth. Nothing else moved in the vicinity except the rain and wind–whipped cottonwood and willow branches.

He stood shivering under the lean-to, watching the river. There was no sign yet of the first of the Stockton packets. He had been there less than five minutes when the ferry bell on the opposite side of Dead Man's Slough began its muted summons. Noah Rideout's transportation to Schyler Island, no doubt. Through the downpour he saw light bloom brighter in the ferryman's shack, then had glimpses of the grizzled tender emerging with a bug-eye lantern in hand and readying the scow. It would be a rough and potentially dangerous crossing in this weather, even though the slough water at that point was not as badly roiled as the open river.

But the ferryman knew his onions. After more than ten minutes, the barge returned to this side without incident. A large hooded carriage drawn by a brace of horses rattled off the lowered apron, came on down the road to the landing. Quincannon stepped out from under the lean-to to meet it. It was a black Concord buggy, gold mono-grammed letters on its body — *NJR* — just visible through the blowing rain. The driver, wearing a hooded oilskin slicker, set the brake and stepped down. Rideout's aide, Foster.

"What are you doing here?" he demanded when he recognized Quincannon.

"The same as you. Waiting for Mr. Rideout."

"I told you he won't want to be disturbed tonight. Your business with him can wait until tomorrow."

"No, it can't."

Foster glared at him. "If you're looking for trouble, mister, you'll find more than you can handle with me."

"I doubt that," Quincannon said. "What I have to say to Mr. Rideout may save him a considerable sum of money —"

He broke off at the sound of the first shrill blast of a packet's whistle. This was followed by two more, which announced her intention to put in at Kennett's Crossing. He stepped back onto the landing, in time to make out the steamer's three tiers of blurred lights downriver. In that moment a lull between gusts brought a new sound to his ears. It was faint and far-off, an odd hollow chunking. Almost immediately it came again . . . and again. It seemed to be coming from on or across the slough, but he couldn't be certain of exactly where. He waited to hear it one more time — and heard only the wind, the harsh slap-and-gurgle of the river water as it punished the landing's pilings and the flanking banks.

Foster was tending to the somewhat skittish horses; he seemed content now to wait for his employer's arrival before saying anything more. The night boat was now making her turn toward Kennett's Crossing. She was within a few hundred yards of the landing, her buckets churning, when a slicker-clad figure came hurrying down the levee road, tacking unsteadily through the mud and rain. He lurched past the buggy onto the landing — the old man with the glass eye, Dana. He was almost upon Quincannon before spying him; he started so violently he came close to losing his balance and toppling into the river.

"Hellfire!" he shouted when he recovered. He leaned close to peer into Quincannon's face, breathing whiskey fumes at him. "That you, you damn Johnny Reb? What you lurking here for?"

"I'm not lurking; I'm waiting for the night boat."

"Frisco bound, eh?"

"No. Meeting someone."

"Another Copperhead, I'll wager." The old man followed this with a lusty belch. "Say, you got relatives fought with the Confederates at Antietam?"

"No. Every member of my family was faithful to the Union."

"Damn lie." Foster had come up onto the landing and Dana appealed to him, "Reb that shot my eye out looked just like this fella here."

Foster said nothing. Quincannon said irritably, "I was eight years old in 1862."

"Phooey." Dana belched again, then moved over to the far end of the shelter to watch the packet's approach.

The steamer's captain was experienced at landing in the midst of a squall. He brought the stern-wheeler in straight to the landing, her whistle shrieking fitfully, and held her there with her buckets lashing the river while a team of deckhands slung out a gangplank. As soon as the plank was down, a man wearing a yellow slicker and rain hat and toting a carpetbag hurried off. After which Dana, with a one-eyed glower at Quincannon and a muttered, "Goddamn all Johnny Rebs," staggered on board. The deckhands immediately hauled in the plank and the steamer swung out toward mid-channel again. The entire operation had taken no more than a minute.

The arriving passenger was Noah Rideout; he went straight to the Concord buggy, where Foster now stood. Quincannon joined them as Foster opened the door and slung the carpetbag inside.

"My name is John Quincannon, Mr. Rideout. Of Carpenter and Quincannon, Professional Detective Services, San Francisco."

"Detective?" Rideout peered up at him; he was half a head shorter and stood with his feet widespread, in a way that was both belligerent and challenging. He reminded Quincannon of a fighting cock.

Foster said, "He came out to the ranch

this afternoon looking for you, sir. Wouldn't tell me why."

"Not true," Quincannon said. "I told him why — Pauline Dupree."

Rideout stiffened visibly. He said nothing for nine or ten seconds while the wind wailed and one of the horses let loose with a mournful whicker. Then, warily, "What about Pauline Dupree?"

"It's a long story. One that may well be advantageous to you, financially and otherwise."

"It's late," Foster said, "and Mr. Rideout is in need of rest. You can tell him your tale tomorrow —"

Rideout said, "Shut up, Caleb," without looking at him. Then, to Quincannon, "Advantageous to me, you said?"

"If your business in Stockton included a meeting with Gus Burgade."

"Who?"

"A barrel of a man wearing a buffalo coat. An emissary of Miss Dupree's."

"Emissary? The hell you say!"

"Then you did have such a meeting. At which you turned over a large amount of cash to him. Correct?"

"By Christ! What are you trying to sell me?"

"Tell, not sell. I am neither a blackmailer

nor an extortionist, though I can't say the same for Miss Dupree."

There was another short pause. "I don't believe it," Rideout said then, but his voice lacked conviction.

"I believe I can prove it to you. Shall we step in out of the rain, sir?"

The rancher turned abruptly to the buggy, shook off Foster's attempt to help him, and drew himself inside. Quincannon followed. Though it was a relief to be shed of the storm, his clothing was saturated and he felt the night's chill deep in his bones. The rain pelting down on the calash hood was loud enough to make conversation almost as difficult as it had been outside.

Rideout noted it, too. "It's too noisy to converse here," he said loudly. "Suppose you come along with me to my farm. I can damn well use a drink while I listen to what you have to say."

"If it wouldn't be an imposition."

"Imposition, hell. You were hoping I would invite you, to save spending the night in that rathole of Adam Kennett's, else you wouldn't have brought your valise along."

Quincannon didn't deny it.

The coach rocked as Foster climbed up into the driver's seat. Rideout shouted up to him, "Move out, Caleb!"

"Now, Mr. Rideout?"

"Now. And don't spare the horses."

The Concord jerked into motion, wheeling away from the landing and onto the muddy levee road. When they reached the ferryman's shack, the muscular tender emerged with his bug-eye lantern. The black scowl he wore testified to his displeasure at having to make two dangerous crossings of Dead Man's Slough on such a night as this. As did his grumbling remark that "the wind is a she-devil tonight, the current flood fast" — the most words Quincannon had heard him speak at once.

Rideout put an end to his protestations with a gold coin that flashed in the light from the bug-eye lantern. The ferryman had the apron down and was making ready with the windlass when Foster drove the Concord buggy down the embankment.

The horses were even more skittish now; Foster had some difficulty coaxing them onto the rocking barge. He set the brake and then swung down to hold the animals' harnesses while the ferryman hooked the guard chain, cast off the mooring ropes, and bent to his windlass.

Impulse prodded Quincannon out of the carriage, to stand braced against the off-rear wheel. He disliked being closed inside a conveyance in such situations as this, preferring to be in a position to observe the proceedings and to offer assistance if needed. And he couldn't get any wetter than he already was. He scanned as much of both shores as could be made out through the deluge. He thought he saw someone moving on the road near the town wharf, a dark shape like a huge winged vulture, but he couldn't be sure; very little was distinct in the rain-soaked night.

Progress was slow, the barge rolling and pitching on the turbulent water. They were less than halfway across when Quincannon heard a singing moan in the storm's racket — wind vibrating the ferry cable, he thought, or the strain on the scow produced by the load and the strong current. Suddenly, then, the barge lurched, made a dancing little sideslip that almost tore loose his grip on the buggy's wheel.

The ferryman shouted a warning that the wind shredded away. In the next instant there was a loud snapping noise and something came hurtling through the wet blackness, cracking like a whip. One of the cables, broken free of its anchor on the north bank spit.

Swirling water bit into the scow, drenched Quincannon to the knees as it sluiced across the deck. The ferryman was thrown backward from the windlass; the drum spun free, ratcheting. He shouted again. So did Foster, something unintelligible. The barge, floating loose now and caught by the current, heaved and bucked toward the slough's confluence with the dark sweep of the river.

The terror-stricken horses reared, and one's hoof must have struck Foster; he screamed in pain, staggered, lost his balance, and was gone into the roiling slough. Quincannon felt the deck canting over, the buggy beginning to tip and slide away from him. Rideout had the door open now and was trying to struggle out; Quincannon caught hold of his arm, yanked him free. In another few seconds the carriage would roll and the weight of it and the horses tumbling would capsize the scow. There was nothing to be done but go into the water themselves, attempt to swim clear while they were still in the slough.

The ferryman knew it, too. He yelled a third time — "Jump, jump!" — and dove over the guard chain.

But Rideout fought against going overboard. Clawed desperately to free himself from Quincannon's grasp, to cling to the side rail, all the while shouting, "I can't swim! I can't swim!"

Quincannon was bigger, stronger, younger, and there was no time left for such concerns. He wrenched the farmer around, locked an arm about his waist, and hurled both of them off the tilting deck.

23

QUINCANNON

Rideout's struggles grew frenzied as the icy water closed over them. Quincannon nearly lost his grip on the rancher's slicker, managed to hold on and to kick them both up to the surface and away from the danger behind them. The barge was tilted in the opposite direction; the screams of the horses rose above the storm sounds as it went over, spilling carriage and animals into the slough in a huge foaming gout. The roaring noise this generated had the volume of a thunderclap.

Rideout continued his panicked flailing and sputtering, which left Quincannon no choice in this matter, either. He pulled his right arm free and rapped the man smartly on the chin with a closed fist, a blow that put an abrupt end to the struggle.

The current had them, but it was not half as powerful here as it would be if they were swept into the river. The waterlogged chesterfield was a heavy weight that threatened to drag both of them down; Quincannon ripped the buttons loose, then shucked the right arm out of its sleeve, shifted his grasp on the unconscious Rideout, and worked the left one free.

Quincannon could move more easily then in the churning water, and not a moment too soon. Something bulky and misshapen swirled toward them; he saw it just in time to twist himself and Rideout out of its path. Blasted tree limb torn loose by the storm, a large one sprouting mossy branches. The miss was so close that one of the branches scratched the back of his hand as the limb spun by.

Once it was gone he made an effort to get his bearings. There, over to his left — the faint light at the ferryman's shack. He took a firmer grip on his burden and struck out in that direction.

The wind and the current battled him at every stroke, bobbing the pair of them like corks. Once an eddy almost ripped Rideout away from him. Quincannon's right leg threatened to cramp; the cold and exertion numbed his mind as well as his body. The bank, the light, seemed far away . . . then a little closer . . . and closer still. . . .

It might have been five minutes or fifteen before his outstretched arm finally touched shore mud. He got his feet down, managed to drag himself and his burden up through the silt. Lay there in the pounding rain waiting for his breath and his strength to return.

A shout penetrated the storm, roused him. He sat up weakly. At his side Rideout lay unmoving. A lone figure came staggering toward them from the direction of the ferryman's shack — Foster, also fortunate to have reached the shore.

"Mr. Rideout," he panted as he lurched up to where they were. "My God, he's not —"

"No. Unconscious. The ferryman?"

Foster shook his head. "Gone. Miracle we weren't drowned, too."

While he dropped to one knee beside his employer, Quincannon lifted himself shakily to his feet and felt under his frock coat. Fortunately, the Navy Colt, secure in its holster, had also survived the midnight dunking. Just then there was a new shout and another man, slicker clad, appeared out of the wet darkness. Adam Kennett this time.

"Christ Almighty. You men all right?"

"Lucky to be alive," Quincannon said grimly.

Foster said, "Mr. Rideout must've swallowed a quart or two. I'll get it out of him." He rolled the farmer onto his stomach, straddled him, and began pumping water out of his lungs.

"Where's Granger?" Kennett asked. "Didn't he make it?"

Quincannon was finger-scraping mud out of his beard. "The ferryman? Evidently not."

"Poor old cuss. What happened out there?"

"Cable snapped."

"The hell it did. Granger replaced it just last year. Should have held fast even in a storm like this."

"Freak accident," Foster said.

Bah! Quincannon thought. Attempted murder was more like it. Even the strongest cable could not withstand the blade of an ax. Those hollow chunkings he'd heard earlier had been ax blows. Only one man in Kennett's Crossing was capable of rowing a skiff over to the spit anchor and chopping most of the way through the cable, leaving just enough for the scow to be winched out into midstream before it snapped — Gus Burgade. And there could be just one primary target for such cold-blooded perfidy — John Quincannon.

Foster finished his pumping and got

slowly to his feet. "He'll live if pneumonia doesn't set in."

"We'll take him to the inn," Kennett said, "get him out of those wet clothes and some whiskey and hot coffee into him. Same for both of you."

He and Foster lifted Rideout and carried him up the bank. Quincannon trailed them on legs that were more unsteady than he cared to admit. They slogged along the levee road toward the inn, but as they passed the lane that led to the wharf he veered off onto it. The other two seemed not to notice.

The *Island Star* was as completely light-less as before, her gangplank still lowered and chained to the wharf. He paused to draw his Navy and check the loads. It would be too waterlogged to fire after the soaking in the slough, but if needs be it would serve well enough as a bluff, a bludgeon, or both. Holding it inside his coat, he moved ahead to the gangplank.

No audible sounds came from the old steamer as he boarded her. The hatch leading to the cargo hold and store had been battened down. He went forward, past the now canvas-covered calliope, and climbed to the second deck where the pilothouse and quarters were located. A faint strip of lamplight, undetectable from the shore below, showed from beneath the door to the first cabin. He pressed his ear to the panel, heard nothing from within. The latch yielded to careful pressure; he withdrew the Navy, eased the door open, stepped inside.

Few things surprised Quincannon after all his years as a detective, but the sight that confronted him here was unexpected enough to have that effect. The light came from a lantern fixed to one of the bulkheads, its wick turned down low. In its pallid glow, the two dead men sprawled on the deckboards were like wax figures in a grisly museum display.

One, the kanaka deckhand, lay facedown just to the right of the door, evidently ventilated just after entering. Gus Burgade was the other, propped in a sideways lean against the bulkhead opposite. Both men had been shot, Burgade more than once; blood glistened blackly on his throat and down the front of his linsey-woolsey shirt. There was a Remington double-action revolver in one thick-knuckled hand, drawn too late to save his life. Quincannon holstered his Navy, went to where the body lay, and bent for a closer look at the blood; it was just starting to coagulate. He lifted the revolver, sniffed the muzzle. No powder smell. The only shots that had been fired in here were those that had done for the victims.

A brief visual search of the cabin satisfied him that neither struggle nor search had taken place. His mouth set in grim lines, his freebooter's whiskers bristling, he hurried out and closed the door behind him.

The rain was easing some, a fact he barely noticed as he descended the gangplank. He hurried uphill to the inn. His entrance into the common room, accompanied by a gust of wind and rain, was abrupt enough to startle Adam Kennett and a second person standing before the pulsing heat of the cast-iron woodstove.

The second person was a nun wearing a black habit, scapular, cowl, and veil.

The veil had been raised, revealing a white, middle-aged countenance; she lowered it as Quincannon crossed the room, shaking himself doglike on the way. He stopped near the stove. The nun moved away a few paces to give him her place.

"Well," he said to the innkeeper, "so now I know why you've made this a temporary temperance house. Why didn't you tell me you had a nun staying here?"

"Sister Mary asked me to respect her privacy."

"I did, yes," the nun said. Her voice was a

thin, middle-aged contralto. "I wished to spend the day in my room in meditation and prayer."

"You've not been outside since the storm began, Sister?"

"No. Nor before."

"How long have you been a guest of Mr. Kennett's?"

"Just today and tonight. I shall be leaving for San Francisco in the morning."

"You won't take offense if I say I'm surprised to find a nun in surroundings such as these."

"Not at all. My brother in Walnut Grove is gravely ill, you see. Though no more gravely ill than the poor half-drowned man in the kitchen. I offered a prayer asking God to spare his life."

"Warmer in the kitchen than it is out here," Kennett said. "Foster's watching over him."

"Rideout still unconscious, is he?"

"Yes."

"Are you the good Samaritan who rescued him after the ferry accident?" the nun asked.

"It wasn't an accident," Quincannon said.

Kennett's eyebrows bent upward. "What do you mean, it wasn't an accident?"

"Just that. Attempted murder is what it was, of both myself and, I suspect, Noah

Rideout."

"But . . . who would do such a thing?"

"Gus Burgade."

"Burgade!"

"On his own initiative, perhaps, but more likely on orders."

"Orders? Orders from whom?"

Quincannon moved, ostensibly to stand closer to the stove's warmth. Instead, he veered suddenly to the nun's side and in one swift motion reached up and tore off her cowl and veil.

She gasped and pulled away, pale gold tresses spilling down around her theatrically aged and made-up face.

Kennett released an outraged bleat. "How dare you mistreat a holy woman — !"

"Holy woman? Faugh! She is no more a nun than I am. Her name is Pauline Dupree, an accomplished actress and a cold-blooded multiple murderess. She shot one man to death in San Francisco and two more tonight on the *Island Star.*"

"You son of a bitch!" she cried. Her hand had snaked inside her habit and it re-appeared now clutching a small-caliber pistol. Before she could bring it to bear, Quincannon, who had never before struck a woman, nor ever would except in dire circumstances such as these, essayed a swift right-hand jab to Dupree's jaw. Down she went in a black-and-gold heap, to lie unmoving with her eyes rolled up. He bent to retrieve the pistol, slipped it into his coat pocket.

Kennett's mouth hung open in disbelief. Foster had come running in from the kitchen and he, too, stood gawping.

After a few seconds the innkeeper managed to ask, "Who . . . who the devil are you, Flint?"

"His name isn't Flint," Foster said. "It's Quincannon and he's a fly cop from San Francisco. I heard him tell that to Mr. Rideout."

"A fly cop." Kennett shook his head in a dazed fashion. "And you claim this woman murdered two men on the *Island Star* tonight?"

"Gus Burgade and his deckhand. You'll find them both in Burgade's cabin."

"But . . . *why?*"

"It's a long story," Quincannon said. "Suffice it to say for now that it boils down to a combination of ruthlessness and greed."

Foster asked, "How did you know she wasn't what she pretended to be? Did you recognize her?"

Quincannon had known it from the moment he first saw her, known for several reasons that it was Dupree in another of her theatrical disguises. But this was not the time for lengthy explanations. He said only, "Detective work, gentlemen, of the most accomplished sort." Then, "Fetch a length or two of rope, Mr. Kennett. If we don't truss her up before she comes to, I guarantee we'll have a tigress on our hands."

Kennett fetched the rope and Quincannon did the tying. His handkerchief served as an effective gag. In a pocket of her habit he found and removed her room key; it was unmarked, but the innkeeper provided the number. He directed Kennett and Foster to put the bound woman into one of the cane-bottom chairs, and while this was being done he hurried down the central corridor and let himself into her lamplit room.

The first thing he spied, hung on a wall hook, was the red-and-gold hooded cape she'd worn on the *Captain Weber.* The fabric was dripping wet — further proof, if he'd needed any, that she had gone from the inn to the *Island Star* earlier, no doubt having left unseen by a rear entrance. Her carpetbag lay on the foot on the bed; he opened it, rummaged quickly through the contents without finding what he sought.

In the small wardrobe against one wall? No. Under the bed? Yes.

He dragged out the still damp leather satchel, the same one Burgade had carried into the Yosemite Hotel yesterday, and snapped the catch. Packets of greenbacks filled it to the brim — a larger amount of cash, Quincannon guessed, than the ten thousand dollars Dupree had extorted from Titus Wrixton.

He closed the satchel, took it with him into the common room. Until tomorrow, when the sheriff of Walnut Grove could be summoned, it would remain in Quincannon's possession.

Pauline Dupree had regained her senses and was squirming mightily, and futilely, in the cane-bottom chair. Her face was congested with fury. She glared pure hate at Quincannon when she saw him and the satchel; a lengthy series of strangled sounds erupted from her, trapped by her gag. Few could give vent to a longer, more colorful burst of invective than John Quincannon, but he would have wagered those strangled sounds represented scorch-ear cussing that would have outclassed his by a considerable margin.

24

SABINA

"And so," John said, "you decided not to turn the Japanese girl over to the police."

It was Wednesday morning, John having returned to the city late the previous day, and Sabina had just finished telling him of her investigation and its outcome.

"I felt it was the best choice for all concerned," she said. "Kamiko acted only out of love and loyalty to Amity, and in self-defense at Prudence Egan's hideaway. Justice would not have been served by sending her to prison. In fact, it would have been an act of cruelty. You know as well as I how viciously Orientals can be treated by those on both sides of the law."

"I do. But are you certain the girl won't commit another such crime if her guardian is threatened again?"

"She swore a solemn oath she wouldn't. I believe that, too. Amity has forgiven her and

she'll see to it there are no more incidents."
Sabina paused and then asked, "Do you approve of my decision?"

"Yes. I have implicit trust in your judgment."

She had been sure that he would approve. He shared her belief that in cases such as this justice tempered by compassion was preferable to following the strict letter of the law.

He finger-fluffed his whiskers in that habitual way of his before asking, "Fenton Egan has no idea you wrote the anonymous note that sent him to Larkin Street, I take it?"

"Evidently not, since neither he nor the police have contacted me. According to the newspapers, his wife was the victim of a burglar caught in the act or of an attempted criminal assault. But I wouldn't be surprised if he considers one of her lovers responsible."

"A disreputable fellow, from your description of him."

"As was she. Both adulterers, both mean-spirited."

"And Mrs. Egan having slipped a buckle, to plan to murder her perceived rival in cold blood."

"Yes. And she would have shot Kamiko if

the girl hadn't been able to defend herself."

"What would you have done if Mrs. Egan hadn't been killed? Made your suspicions known to her?"

Sabina had asked herself that question more than once the past few days. "I suppose I would have," she said, "barring any other alternative. I had no real evidence against her, but the knowledge I did possess and a vow to make it public might have been enough to frighten her into never trying it again. The ploy might have worked, depending on how determined she was, and how unbalanced. Fortunately, it's a moot point. Amity's only concern now is that her husband will find out about the affair."

"Do you think Egan is still vindictive enough to inform him?"

"It's possible, but I doubt it. His wife's death and the discovery of her infidelities is all the scandal he's equipped to deal with."

John had flicked a lucifer alight and was applying the flame to the bowl of his briar, puffing out billows of gray-white smoke. Sabina made a mental note to try once again to convince him to change his brand of tobacco to one less odious.

"Kamiko," he said. "Did you suspect her all along?"

"Not exactly. I had an inkling that she

might have alerted Prudence Egan, but it wasn't until I discovered the woman's body and the broken *kaiken* tip that I knew for certain."

"Would you have accused the girl if it weren't for that?"

"Yes. Faced with the fact that I knew the truth, she would have confessed as she did on Sunday morning. And Amity was entitled to know."

He nodded, still puffing. "Never withhold vital information from a client unless absolutely necessary."

"Particularly not if the client is also a friend."

"Mrs. Wellman must be an estimable person, despite her temporary lapse in judgment, to have forgiven her ward so readily."

"She is."

"You'll have to introduce me to her one day."

"I intend to. You'll like her and I think she'll like you." Then, with a twinkle in her eye, "You'll have to come bicycling with us some Sunday."

"Faugh! Bicycling with members of a women's riding club? That day will never dawn in this lad's life."

"There is nothing unmanly in the sport, John."

"Perhaps not. But it's of no interest to me."

"Not even in a good cause? Amity is planning a bicycle rally to help fund Voting Rights for Women."

"I'll offer my support in other ways, if you don't mind."

"Financial support?"

"Well . . . yes, up to a point."

"So you do sincerely believe in our cause."

"I've said so often enough, haven't I? My word is my bond. There is nothing I would like more than to have the women of California given the vote."

Sabina could tell that he meant it. She said, smiling, "Except, that is, for greenbacks and gold specie."

"Speaking of which," he said without missing a beat, "I trust you charged Mrs. Wellman an appropriate fee for all you did for her."

Same old John. Yes, and she supposed she wouldn't have him any other way.

QUINCANNON

"And so," Sabina said, "Pauline Dupree is in custody in Walnut Grove."

It was Wednesday morning, and he had just finished regaling her with an account of his adventures on the *Captain Weber* and in

Stockton and Kennett's Crossing and his hair-breadth escape from drowning in Dead Man's Slough.

"Yes," he said, "and soon to be transferred to the jail in Stockton. Charged with two counts of murder and one of extortion."

"I don't suppose she confessed?"

"No. She refused to speak to me. Or to the Walnut Grove sheriff, once I turned her over to him, except to demand the services of a San Francisco lawyer."

"Which one?"

"She wasn't particular. Whichever one she chooses, I'll hear from him eventually. Not that he'll have any luck in getting her off, despite her considerable charms."

"The charges against her are provable, then."

"Eminently so. The pistol she used to dispatch Gus Burgade and his deckhand was in her possession, as was the twelve thousand dollars she obtained from Noah Rideout through her pawn, Burgade. Not a man to be trifled with, Mr. Rideout. Once informed of her deceit, he couldn't wait to bring the extortion charges against her."

Quincannon favored Sabina with a well-pleased smile. "And he was so grateful for my having saved his life, his twelve thousand dollars, and his reputation from considerable embarrassment that he presented me with a handsome reward." He saw no need to add that the reward had been his idea, not Rideout's, and that it had come only after a bit of verbal tussling.

"How handsome?" Sabina asked.

"Five hundred dollars. His check is in my purse, soon to be deposited in our account at the Miners Bank."

Sabina ran the pink tip of her tongue over her lips, a mannerism that never failed to spark Quincannon's imagination. "What about the money Dupree extorted from Titus Wrixton?" she asked. "Did she have that in her possession as well?"

"No. She sent the cash on ahead to New York by Wells Fargo Express."

"How do you know that?"

"I found the receipt in her bag. Along with a one-way ticket on the transcontinental train from Sacramento and a packet of highly indiscreet letters Rideout had written to her, which I returned to him."

Sabina shook her head. "Why men insist on writing such overheated *billets-doux* is beyond me."

"Love does strange things to some people," Quincannon said sagely. He himself had never penned such missives, nor even once been tempted to. Actions, after all, spoke louder and more passionately than words.

"Did she also have Wrixton's letters?"

"No. She may have destroyed them. More likely, knowing her devious and duplicitous ways, she intended to keep them and the ones from Rideout, as insurance in the event she ever again needed large sums of money. If that's the case, it's probable she sent the banker's missives on ahead with his ten thousand dollars. The cash, if not the letters, will be recovered and handed over to Wrixton; I'll see to that."

"When do you intend to inform him of her arrest?"

"This afternoon," Quincannon said. "The sheriff provided me with a signed deposition proving that she's in custody and outlining the charges against her. That should be sufficient to convince even a love-blind mooncalf that he was bamboozled."

"And to allow you to collect the balance of the fee he owes."

"Oh, he'll pay it, and without another peep of protest, or I'll take it from his blasted bank and frame him for embezzlement."

"Really, John . . ."

"Merely a figure of speech, my dear," he assured her, more or less honestly. "But I've earned that fee balance three times over and nearly lost my life in the process. I won't be denied."

Sabina had a few more questions. "When do you suppose Dupree found out that you were on her trail?" she asked.

"When I first arrived at Kennett's Inn. She was cosseted in her room at the time, the one nearest the common room, and likely she overheard my conversation with Adam Kennett."

"It must have given her quite a shock."

"Undoubtedly," Quincannon said with relish. "She must have also overheard my later mention to the innkeeper that I intended to meet Noah Rideout at the steamer landing. It was she who put Burgade up to taking an ax to the ferry's cable, shortly before she disposed of him and his unfortunate deckhand."

"How did you know so quickly that it was Dupree in the nun's habit? You said her makeup and the use of cotton wadding to change the shape of her mouth and cheeks made for another flawless impersonation."

"Several reasons. First, she had to be in Kennett's Crossing that night; no one else had a better motive for disposing of her cohort in the Rideout extortion. Second, her skill at playacting a variety of different roles. Third, the figure I saw hurrying away from the store boat shortly before the ferry cable snapped. In the rainy darkness a woman wearing a wind-blown garment could well resemble a huge winged vulture. And fourth, a nun passed through the lobby of the Yosemite Hotel during my vigil — a curious sight in retrospect, for nuns usually travel in pairs. Dupree in her nun's disguise, the habit brought with her from San Francisco." He added, somewhat ruefully, that he had also paid scant attention to the carpetbag the nun was carrying, a fact he'd recalled only after he'd yaffled her. There had been nothing distinctive about her bag, and many guests had toted similar luggage in and out of the hotel lobby.

"But why was she wearing the disguise then?" Sabina asked. "Did she intend to pose as a nun all the way to New York?"

"More likely only as far as Sacramento. My deduction is that Burgade had been charged with bringing Mr. Rideout's twelve thousand dollars to her at the hotel and that she had plans to cosh him or dope his drink in her room and then make off with the loot in her nun's disguise. But he double-crossed her. The note he wrote and had sent up to her room must have been a demand for a larger cut of the spoils and that she meet him on Sunday in Kennett's Crossing to make the exchange. A fool as well as a knave, Burgade. That note was his death warrant."

"And she wore her nun's disguise when she left the hotel for the same purpose, to make Pauline Dupree disappear into thin air from that point onward."

"My surmise as well," he agreed. "She could then travel to Kennett's Crossing and commit her crimes there with impunity before moving on to Sacramento. Or so she thought, not having reckoned on the doggedness and cunning of John Frederick Quincannon."

25

SABINA

On Friday evening John escorted her to a performance of Verdi's *Aida* at the Opera House, followed by a late supper of oysters *a la poulette* at the Poodle Dog.

It was a splendid evening. He was quite handsome in his evening clothes and top hat, his thick beard more neatly trimmed than usual. (She'd overhead a woman whisper to her companion at the opera house that Sabina's electric-blue-and-black ruffled gown was stunning and that she and John made a very attractive couple.) And he'd been a perfect gentleman, managing to remain alert during the entire performance and to not once mention business matters or money during dinner. Even the weather cooperated. The fog and drizzle of the previous few days had given way to clear skies and a significant rise in temperature. Spring had finally arrived in the city.

Most satisfying of all, though, was simply having John back safe and sound. She'd missed his company, even missed his idiosyncrasies and minor irritants. Missed him more than she cared to admit. Well, no, that wasn't true. Why not admit it? Indeed, why not? After all, hadn't she conceded to herself not so long ago that her time with him had wrought a profound change in her feelings toward him, that inside his crusty shell he was as kind, as considerate, as doting, as Stephen had been during their courtship and all-too-brief marriage . . . ?

". . . coffee, Sabina?"

She blinked and looked up. "Hmm?"

"I asked if you'd like more coffee?"

"Oh. No, I've had plenty."

"You seem a bit . . . distracted. Not enjoying yourself?"

"On the contrary. I was just doing a bit of woolgathering."

"About what?"

"Oh, this and that." She smiled. "Let's be on our way now, shall we?"

Outside John took her arm and led her to a waiting hansom. When they were seated inside, he leaned forward to speak to the driver, but she placed a restraining hand on his arm.

"It occurs to me," she said in lowered

tones, "that I have never been to your flat."

He said blankly, "My flat?"

"You've never described it and I'm curious. I should like to see it."

". . . You would? When?"

"Now. Tonight."

In the light from the cab's interior lamp, John's jaw hung agape like a puppet's; for once he was utterly speechless. It was Sabina who had to give his Leavenworth Street address to the driver.

AUTHORS' NOTE

There was in fact a California State Woman Suffrage Convention held in San Francisco in November of 1896. Its delegates wore badges such as the one described here, and the campaign was in fact headed by Susan B. Anthony. Unfortunately, her tireless efforts and those of dedicated proponents such as Sabina and Amity Wellman were in vain. The proposed amendment to the state constitution giving women the right to vote was soundly defeated, owing in large part to the powerful Liquor Dealers League and the considerable clout the organization wielded with both Democratic and Republican politicians. It was not until 1911, thanks to a new, more widespread, more determined suffragist movement risen phoenix-like from the ashes of the 1906 earthquake, that California women were finally granted voting rights.

Steamboats were still a primary mode of

transportation between San Francisco and Stockton in 1896. The *Captain Weber* was an actual stern-wheeler that made the daily overnight run; the descriptions herein of her route and her physical characteristics are as accurate as research can make them. Also as stated, the stern-wheeler was operated by the Union Transportation Company and owned by Sarah Gillis, widow of the original owner and an ardent member of the Stockton branch of the Woman's Christian Temperance Union; thus, the *Captain Weber* and her sister boat, the *Dauntless,* were the only two dry packets on the San Joaquin River. There were none on the Sacramento River.

In the closing years of the century several small hamlets and enclaves did dot the islands of the delta, among them Rye and the settlement of Locke, founded by Chinese who toiled as farm laborers. Kennett's Crossing, however, while representative of these isolated communities and their citizens, exists only in our fevered imaginations.

M.M. / B.P.

ABOUT THE AUTHORS

Marcia Muller is the *New York Times* bestselling creator of private investigator Sharon McCone. The author of more than thirty-five novels, Muller received the MWA's Grand Master Award in 2005.

Bill Pronzini, creator of the Nameless Detective, is a highly praised novelist, short story writer, and anthologist. He received the Grand Master Award from the MWA in 2008, making Muller and Pronzini the only living couple to share the award.